The Other Side of the Mirror

Detective Duarte Mysteries

Book 1

Dyslexia Friendly Edition

Jamie Sands

ROOKERY

ROOKERY PUBLISHING

New Zealand

Text set in OpenDyslexicAlta

- ISBN 978-0-473-60468-4 (Softcover - POD)
- ISBN 978-0-473-60472-1 (Softcover - POD Amazon)
- ISBN 978-0-473-60470-7 (Epub)
- ISBN 978-0-473-60471-4 (Kindle)
- ISBN 978-0-473-60469-1 (Hardcover - POD)

Contents

Prologue

Daniel took the path from the road to his grandmother's house. His eyes were on his phone, he knew this route so well he didn't need to pay much attention to his feet.

He rang the doorbell and flicked off another message to his boyfriend, Joe.

Bae, miss you so much <3

He waited a few minutes. The door didn't open so he sent a couple of emojis and saw the three dots bouncing as Joe typed his response.

Miss you too! xoxo

He smiled, took a selfie of the smile, and sent it back. Daniel loved posting selfies but they were curated to make him look a bit tougher, a bit edgier. Joe got the smiles. Only Joe, and

Jamie Sands

under threat of severe pain if he ever shared them with anyone.

Daniel pocketed his phone and knocked on the door. Had the doorbell actually sounded? It could be broken. He couldn't remember hearing the chime, but maybe he'd ignored it.

He peered in the window beside the door. No sign of her approaching.

He sighed, he'd have to let himself in. Gran would tease him about being young and impatient or something like that.

He cupped his hands to peer through the window again, something was wrong. He couldn't see anything, only the empty living room. A cup sat by her usual chair.

The newspaper was folded up to show the crossword. Her pen sat on top of the paper, like she'd been sitting there and had meant to come back.

Maybe she'd gone out? But she'd known he was coming over and she always made sure to be home. She'd even texted a couple of hours ago. She'd sent it while he'd been in his last lecture for the day.

He reached for the key she kept hidden on top of the window frame next to the door. He had to go up on the tiptoes of his battered black Chuck Taylors and stretch, but he found it. Damn tall grandmother.

He stuck the key into the lock and opened the door.

"Gran? It's Daniel." He moved into the house. He glanced at the row of hooks on the left, the plaque on top read 'Happy Home', and he recognised her keys by the best grandma keyring he'd given her when he was ten. She hadn't gone out. "Are you in the bathroom?"

The house was silent. But there was a smell. Something burning.

Jamie Sands

He went into the kitchen. "Gran? Gran, are you okay?"

The kitchen was empty. He switched the oven off, opened the door, and inside was a batch of... somethings. Once cookies, but they'd gone a bit black around the edges. His stomach dropped away unpleasantly. No way would Gran walk out on cookies baking. She prided herself on having fresh baking when company came around. Ever since she'd retired, she'd been passionate about baking.

He pulled out his phone and turned around, looking closer at the kitchen. Yep, definitely empty. The baking dishes were half done in the sink, the water murky. He stuck a finger into the dishwater. The water wasn't entirely cold. His stomach knotted itself.

The fuck had happened? The kitchen was pristine usually, carefully organised with everything in its place. If there were unfinished dishes, then she'd been interrupted.

"Gran? Gran!" His throat was tight, and it made his voice sound strained. He checked the rest of the house. She wasn't in the bathroom. Not in the bedroom. Not in the tidy, well-organised garage. Not in her little energy-efficient car. Not in the laundry room. Not in the guest bedroom. "Gran!"

He opened the back door and checked the yard. The beds of vegetables and carefully tended roses were the same as he'd seen them last. The bench he'd been meaning to paint sat under the apple tree, empty.

His phone buzzed in his hand. He looked at it, but it was another message from Joe. No time for that. He dialled the emergency number and slammed the phone to his ear, going back inside to do another patrol, checking inside cupboards and closets, just in case.

"Hello? I need the police. My gran's missing."

"Certainly, what's your name?"

Jamie Sands

"Daniel Armstrong. The address is 895 Moana Ave, One Tree Hill. Please, I don't know where she is." He poked his head into the bedroom again and frowned. There was something there he hadn't noticed before, or that hadn't been there before.

"I understand, we'll help you. Please stay on the line and let us know when you last saw her."

He moved into the bedroom and looked at the bed. There was an indentation on the perfectly made covers, like someone had recently been having a lie-down. In the middle of the indentation was a yellowed piece of paper, there was something written on it. The hairs on the back of his neck rose, but he couldn't resist the urge to know what the paper said.

"What?" He breathed, not even thinking about the voice on the other end of the phone.

"What did you say? Daniel? Please, can you tell me when you last saw your grandmother, and what her name is?"

He let his hand fall to his side, his phone held loosely. The paper read: *A debt is paid.*

1

Jack sat in the break room trying to make herself care enough to read the newspaper. It wasn't working. The newspaper was full of smarmy politicians doing shitty things, community news like 'local kid managed to save some bees', and horoscopes.

It wasn't any of it useful.

She wished she'd brought in her novel but she didn't want anyone to see the title of the book she was reading. She'd spent years cultivating a tough reputation, only to have one of her workmates notice her reading a romance novel and spread it around the office. Everyone had made a big deal about tough Jack and her happy ever after endings.

The worst thing was that the guy cops all read the most obvious airport bookshop bestsellers: Lee Child, Stephen

King, James Patterson. Thrillers, horrors, and police dramas. Then they'd complain about the inaccuracies and the far-fetched plot points. Those books usually had neatly wrapped-up endings as well. But Jack's books had women on the cover and cute fonts and therefore it was hilarious that she read them.

Heaven forbid she be good at her job *and* read for pleasure.

What would they say if they knew she read fanfiction, because at least in those the queer couples ended up together and usually no one died?

She did get sick of them making fun. Between this and the nickname for the cases she took, it got tiring. Jack at least got her own back by solving cases or doing enough legwork that even the unsolved cases she filed were agreed to be unsolvable by anyone who read them. Jack's statistics and solves were unrivalled in the station. So they could make fun of her if they wanted, but she knew she was more effective than any of them.

She pulled up a fanfiction website on her phone browser and scrolled through her favourite pairings, pausing when she heard footsteps.

Coleson walked in and gave her a knowing smile. "Duarte."

"What is it?" Jack sighed and sat up, locking her phone, pushing her in-need-of-a-trim fringe back off her face and folding her arms so she could properly glare at him. Pushing her hair back from her face was a tic she couldn't be bothered correcting. She did it when she was annoyed, confused, or uncertain. In this case, it was in annoyance.

Coleson was what was usually called 'old school' by the same people who'd say 'boys will be boys.' Tall, he had at least six inches on Jack and seemed to enjoy reminding her of that. He was white, greying a little, and enjoyed making her life hell for no apparent reason. Or maybe the reason was as simple as Jack was a woman and a good cop.

"Case came in, has your name written all over it."

Jack frowned. "My name?"

Coleson's Hollywood–bad guy smirk made her fist itch to punch him.

"Locked room mystery. An old lady vanished, her house looking like the *Mary Celeste*. You know, the ghost ship?"

"Yes, Coleson, I've heard of the *Mary Celeste*."

"You've probably tried to *solve* the *Mary Celeste*." He chuckled. Jack glared. Yes, of course she'd tried to solve the empty ship adrift mystery. It was fascinating stuff. But she wouldn't let him know that.

"Are you going to tell me about this case?"

Jamie Sands

"No evidence except a three-word note and a hysterical gay grandson."

"You don't have to specify he's gay," she said automatically. She got up. "It's hardly pertinent to what you're telling me."

Coleson folded his arms and stood in her way. "Another weird-ass case for our very own ghost hunter."

"I'm not a ghost hunter," Jack muttered before she could stop herself and glared extra hard at him for baiting her. *Damnit.* Now it was going to be her new nickname.

"Ghost Hunter Duarte," Coleson said, drawing it out like he was a kid with a new... she didn't even know. A fidget spinner, maybe?

"Get out of my way, Coleson," she growled, so he'd know he'd better move. She was pleased when he did step away. She might have a reputation for picking up weird cases, but she also had a reputation for taking no shit.

The break room was on the opposite side of the station to the detective rooms, and up the hall from the sergeant's private office. Jack turned into the hallway and saw the sergeant waiting for her outside her office, arms folded, finger tapping against her bicep. Jack quickened her pace.

"Duarte, where were you?"

"On my lunch break." Jack followed her into her office.

Sergeant Brie Apanui was a formidable woman. Jack had admired her from the moment she'd walked into the station with the job. She wore severe but beautifully tailored suits – skirts or trousers depending on the weather – and kept her hair natural, curling around her shoulders or wrapped in a headscarf.

Jack had never had the patience to wear suits herself, but she'd updated her work wardrobe from T-shirts and jeans to collared shirts and chinos once Apanui had become her boss.

Jamie Sands

Jack didn't have the same strong shoulders or physical presence of Apanui. Her body tended to slightness and she had to work hard for any muscles she had.

Apanui was formidable in her manner as well. She wasn't a person you wanted to start an argument with, which was lucky because with people like Coleson in the station you needed a firm hand in charge. She was also fair, which Jack appreciated. Jack probably wouldn't be allowed to specialise in the weird cases she had in another station, with another sergeant.

"Don't bother sitting, we don't have much to go on, it won't take long."

"Right." Jack stood, trying not to feel like she was all elbows, impossible in the presence of such a graceful and poised woman.

"Missing persons, Edith Armstrong. Seventy-eight years old. Retired. She used to work for the Auckland City Council in an admin role of some kind." Apanui passed the folder to Jack.

Jack took the folder and flipped straight to the photo. It showed an old white woman whose expression was serious but there were smile lines etched into the skin around her eyes. Her hair was grey, permed with a slight blue rinse, and her eyes were a bright brown. She reminded Jack of one of the teachers at one of her primary schools, a matriarchal figure who was kind to Jack, coming in as a new kid.

"She was supposed to be home to meet her grandson yesterday afternoon but the house was empty. No evidence of a struggle, the stove was on with cookies burning inside, and a weird note left on her bed. The officers have photographed everything. There's one more thing before you go."

Jamie Sands

Jack raised her eyes from the photo to look at Apanui.

"Something else?"

"You're taking a partner."

Jack's mind raced. A partner?

When she was already the whole station's punchline? She'd managed to get along okay, had gotten used to it at least, but to bring someone new on would be like career suicide. For them.

"I am not," Jack said. Apanui raised an eyebrow and Jack looked down, biting her tongue. "Sorry, Sergeant."

"You are taking the new transfer from Central. Their name is Piper Gage."

"Their name?"

"Mm-hm, they're non-binary and their pronouns are they and them. They've been on the force for a couple of years down

South, Christchurch Central. Mostly relegated to rescuing chickens and cats out of trees, that kind of work. As I understand it, there were some problems down there."

"Problems?" Jack shifted her weight onto her other foot. She wanted to sit down but Apanui had explicitly said not to.

"Yes, some interpersonal complaints. I've met Piper. I don't think there's anything in this but internal politics and a healthy dose of bigotry. The way they're written up looks bad. Most likely, it's a case of the bullies getting their records in before the bullied. But it's on file, and I've not been able to offer Piper a full role. It's probation for now, and Human Resources will step in if anything up here goes wrong."

Jack frowned. If this person had been putting up with workplace bullying already, the last thing they needed was to add on Scooby-Doo and X-Files jokes.

Jamie Sands

"Why me?"

"They requested the transfer up here, I accepted. They asked to be partnered with you by name. They're excited. *Highly* excited."

Jack's heart thumped. So, now it was a case of 'match up the queer cops' as well as putting the newbie into the firing line by making them work the kooky cases with Jack.

"Please, Sergeant, I work so much better alone. If you pair them with me the others will pick on them, they'll make fun the way they do me. It won't be a good career move."

Apanui turned to her computer screen. "Not negotiable. They're waiting for you in the main office. You can't miss them."

Jack sighed and shoved the folder under her arm. "I don't know what you expect me to do with an excited newbie."

"Easy. Don't get them killed. Don't kill them. Let them help you. You can delegate to them, remember. They're with you to learn, maybe you can teach them a little about dealing with insufferable male cops. Close the door on your way out." Apanui's eyes were on her screen and there was nothing to do but go. Jack knew her arguments would fall flat.

Jack gave Apanui a weary salute and left.

2

Piper couldn't believe their luck.

They were sitting on a chair next to Detective Duarte's desk. They'd managed to restrain themselves from sitting in her chair and going through every single one of her things. But from where they were sitting, they could see the photograph of a serious-looking man in military uniform who had to be Jack's father.

The others in the office had been making fun of Piper, in a low-key way.

"Signed up with spooky, have you? Hope you're not afraid of the bogeyman."

"Like the idea of living in a horror movie, huh? Well, good luck. You know she's never kept a partner longer than a week."

"Looking forward to calls at two in the morning about conspiracy theories, I hope. You know she believes in chemtrails and monsters under the bed, right?"

Good-natured teasing about the work and about Jack's reputation were fine. If people weren't making fun of Piper about their gender identity or messing up their pronouns on purpose it was an improvement on their old station.

Well, and the other improvement was here they'd get put on actual cases. No more sitting by the side of the road with a speed radar gun. No more chasing a chicken that had escaped from someone's backyard. No more early-morning shifts on the front desk.

Working with Jack was going to be amazing!

Jack had an amazing solve record, even with the weird stuff, and the cases all sounded so freaking interesting. Piper couldn't wait to sink their teeth into the intricacies of what Jack did, and how she approached her cases.

It didn't matter at all what the other officers thought about it, or what they said. Piper could ignore that if they were working a real job with a proper detective. They would prove they could do more police work. They had to. Apanui had promised a review as soon as they'd solved their first case. The outcome of that review could be wonderful, or it could be a ticket back to Christchurch.

"Here she comes," an officer sitting behind Piper said. "Hold on to your skinny jeans."

Piper stood up, brushed off said grey skinny jeans, and adjusted the hem of their formal blue button-up shirt.

Jack was unmistakable. She had a short haircut, and her dark hair fell forward in a long fringe, which was swept to one side. Her eyes were intense, pale blue and striking. Her lips were full but her mouth was set in an annoyed line.

In fact, Jack had the same expression Piper imagined a die-hard cat person would wear after they'd been told they had to adopt a dog. Jack clearly hadn't wanted a partner, but. Piper'd been expecting this. Jack made her way towards her desk and Piper stuck out a hand to her.

"I'm Piper Gage, I'm your new partner. It's a real pleasure to meet you, Detective. I'm a big fan of all your work and I think we'll be really great together."

Jack sighed, tossed a manila folder onto her desk, and gave Piper's hand a quick shake. Her hand was dry, not too warm, and the grip was firm. There was a jangling noise. Piper glanced down to see a silver charm bracelet on Jack's wrist.

"Let's get one thing straight," Jack said. Piper looked up to meet her eye. "I didn't ask for a partner, and generally my partners give up after a week or so. The rest of the station's gonna give you shit for working with me, so you've got to be able to let it slide off your back. I'm gonna do my job pretty much the same way as I would anyway and you can tag along. Got it?"

"Got it," Piper nodded and grinned wide.

Jack narrowed her eyes and shook her head slightly. "Why are you so pleased?"

"It was exactly what I imagined you'd say to me! Word for word, it was as if you were Sam Spade or something. I loved it!" Piper pressed their hands to their chest and quickly dropped them so they didn't look like a cartoon character with hearts for eyes.

Jack blinked at them. "Okay, good?"

Piper smiled. Surprising Jack was almost as good as impressing Jack, wasn't it? "So, what's in the file?"

"Missing persons case. We need to go and look at the house, read up on the victim's history, and talk to the grandson." She ran a hand through her short, scruffy hair and fixed Piper with another look. A calculating one. "Which do you think we should do first?"

Piper licked their lips, thinking fast. "Look at the house, before the evidence gets stale."

"Stale? The officers have already been through and photographed everything."

"Still," Piper said. They nodded, certain of this now. "The grandson will have recorded his statement which we can listen to before we talk to him. He won't forget things, it'll be vivid for him. The house, though, the more people who go through it the more likely something might be stepped on or messed up or looked over and lost."

"Good answer." Jack picked her stab-proof vest from the back of her chair and put it on. Piper hauled theirs out and fastened it on as well. "We'll head to the house first and see what we can see. You drive?'

"Yes, ma'am," Piper said. "I earned full marks on high-speed chase simulations and fast reaction testing."

"You don't need to call me ma'am. In fact, please don't." Jack led the way down to the garage. "Jack is fine."

"Jack. Got it." Jack wasn't taller than them, but Piper had to hurry to keep up. They were out of breath when they arrived at the plain-clothed police car Jack unlocked.

"I'll drive for now, since I'm not in the throes of another whiskey hangover."

"Does that happen often?" Piper asked, feeling a thrill of concern. Piper didn't know Jack well enough to know if it was honesty or dry humour.

"No. I just figured, if you're thinking Sam Spade that'd be in character." Jack gave Piper a brief smile. Dry humour then, Piper smiled.

"Is this your regular car?"

"I use whatever they give me, week to week." Jack climbed into the driver's seat and started the car. Piper hopped in on the passenger side and fastened their safety belt. "I've had this one almost a month now so I'm probably due for a replacement."

Piper ducked down to check the car's supplies in the well.

"It's a standard set up," Jack said. "Gun safes with Glocks under your feet. Boot has Hard Shell armour."

"Cool. So you have a private car as well?"

"No need." Jack backed them out of the garage faster than felt safe. Definitely faster than Piper would have driven.

Jamie Sands

They put a hand on the door to brace. "You ever run a missing persons case before, Piper?"

"No ma'am. Uh, Jack."

Piper smiled to themself, pulled out their phone and checked in with their mother.

First day on the new job, going great! Got a missing persons case with my new partner.

"You texting?" Jack said, sounding impatient.

"Uh, yeah. I'm messaging my mum."

"Keep the details sparse, okay?"

"The details?"

"Of what we're doing. And about me. I'd rather your mum didn't go telling stories to her friends. I know my name's in the news a fair bit. Especially with a missing persons case, you never know who knows who."

Piper raised their eyebrows. It made sense Jack would be paranoid, but about gossip? They lifted their phone, surely Jack wouldn't mind a selfie. They lined up the shot, themselves in the foreground, and Jack behind. She glanced over, then raised a hand off the steering wheel to block her face.

"Nope. No photos, thanks, not unless I say it's all right. No social media about me. In fact, if you're going to do anything, ask me first."

"Anything?" Piper drummed their fingers on the passenger side door and tried to channel their annoyance into teasing. "How about if I want to go to the bathroom? Or pick up a burger? Should I ask you first?"

Jamie Sands

"How about," Jack said, glancing sideways at Piper, "we make the car a place of silent contemplation?"

Piper twisted their mouth to the side and put their phone away. "Fine."

3

Edith's house was a turn-of-the-century, villa-style cottage. There was a fence, a path, and a tidy deck; lots of potted plants and well-tended grass. Inside the house there were polished wooden floors and white-painted walls; framed black-and-white photos hung alongside motel-style landscape prints. The décor was very grandmotherly, florals and comfortable chairs, but the white walls and the new fittings in the kitchen showed it'd been renovated not too long ago, giving it a modern feel.

Jack didn't need much time in the house, apparently. Piper followed behind her, watching, bouncing on the balls of their feet as she skimmed over things Piper might have lingered on. Their eyes were wide, and their heart was racing. This whole thing was so exciting. They couldn't quite handle it.

Jamie Sands

"Look at this!" Piper moved towards a tall wooden dresser. It had shelves displaying various treasures. Snow globes of various tourist destinations: Vegas, Hawaii, Bali, the Cook Islands, ceramic animals and figures and framed photographs.

"What am I looking at?" Jack appeared behind them, her presence shot a shiver up Piper's spine. They squared their shoulders.

"The photos, they could be leads, right? If this Grandma—"

"Edith, use her name," Jack cut in, giving Piper a sharp look. Piper inhaled before speaking again, gathering their courage.

"Right, sorry. If Edith disappeared because someone had a grudge, or whatever, then maybe it's someone in one of these pictures. Crimes are usually committed for personal reasons, right? Usually victims know the perpetrators." Piper took a deep breath and hoped that had sounded intelligent. They'd used enough big words, surely.

Jack nodded. "Not bad. Take photos of the photos. Hopefully the grandson can give us names and save you some time chasing details down."

Piper smiled and took careful photos of each of the framed pictures. Success! Jack was totally impressed and they hoped she thought Piper was a good detective.

"The neighbours have all said she was a lovely person, easy to get along with, no complaints," said a voice Piper didn't recognise. They looked over to see who it was, phone still held up to take the last picture.

Jack frowned, arms folded as she didn't quite make eye contact with the person in the latex gloves and protective gear of a forensics officer.

"I thought you were all done here and it was clear for us to come take a look," Jack said, through gritted teeth.

"Maybe I wanted to hang about to see you." The forensics officer pulled her face mask down and gave Jack a smile. Piper moved the phone to take a photo, but their eyes stayed riveted on Jack and this new woman. Rules be damned, someone was flirting with Jack.

"I don't want to see you, Marlo. I feel I've been quite clear on that point." Jack reached her hand up and pushed her floppy fringe back off her face.

Marlo was tall, and her face was heart shaped and sweet looking. But her tone didn't match the sweetness of her appearance.

"Oh, you're playing with your hair," Marlo said, in a tone dripping with amusement. "I must've made you uncomfortable."

"No, you've pissed me off." Jack folded her arms again, tighter this time, and glared up at the taller woman.

For a moment the two women stared at each other, Marlo smirking and Jack staring back, unwavering. Piper imagined sparks flying in the air between them like they did between cartoon characters.

Finally, Marlo looked away.

"Fine. You have my number if you change your mind. You know where to find me."

"In the forensics lab, next to the morgue? Next to your people?" Jack asked.

Piper sucked in their breath. Marlo pulled her shoulders back and left, brushing past Piper as if she hadn't noticed they were there at all. Once the door slammed, Piper breathed again.

"Who was that?"

"None of your business," Jack said. She ran a hand through her hair and shook her head, allowing her hair to immediately flop forward.

"Sorry, yes. She's gorgeous." Jack shot Piper a look akin to a petrifying glance from Medusa but thankfully didn't turn Piper to stone. "Right, none of my business. Got it." Piper turned back to the dresser and busied themselves photographing everything including the ceramic figure of a shepherdess – not because it was likely to be useful, but because Piper didn't want to meet Jack's gaze anymore.

Behind them, Jack was stomping and moving things around.

Piper went to join Jack where she stood in the bedroom. They both regarded the bed.

It hadn't been touched. The indent in the middle of the bed was clear, as if someone had lain there for a while. In the centre sat the piece of paper. Police tape framed the bed, like a magical barrier keeping it from being disturbed.

"*A debt is paid,*" Piper read.

"That's what it says." Jack's voice was dry as a desert. She cleared her throat and sounded a bit more patient when she continued. "Obviously, this is what we were supposed to find, so... I wouldn't necessarily take it literally. It could easily be a misdirect."

"Do you think she's dead?" Piper asked. It felt like the room had gotten darker somehow. Piper rubbed their arm. Maybe it felt colder? They watched as Jack circled around the far side of the bed.

"I hope not. I'd rather have a win, wouldn't you?" Jack gave Piper a look. "A win would likely help with your probation."

"You know about that?" Piper felt their stomach sink. Somehow they'd hoped that little piece of information had been kept from Jack. That Jack wouldn't be thinking of them as a kind of trouble-making loose cannon.

Even if trouble-making loose cannons sounded cool in books and movies, in real life, in your job, it wasn't a good thing to be.

Jack bent at the waist and took a closer look at the piece of paper, pulling out a pen to lift it away from the bed and check underneath.

"Apanui mentioned something."

Piper looked away, chewing their lip. "So, what do you think happened?"

"I have no idea. We don't have enough information yet."

"But it's weird, right?"

"It's weird. Let's go talk to the boy."

4

Jack and Piper found Daniel in the back garden of the house. He'd already given his official statement and was waiting for an escort home when they came to talk to him. Jack felt for the boy, he was young and this was a very intense situation to find himself in.

Daniel seemed nervous, his left leg kept jiggling. He looked younger than twenty years old; like the fear had de-aged him a little. His eyes were large and wide with worry. His hair was short, with a professional fade shaved into the back and sides. Jack grabbed a folding chair and pulled it over. Piper sat on the wooden bench beside him.

Piper pointed to Jack. "So, she's going to be the bad cop. I'm Piper, I'll be the good one. Do you want another drink?"

"I'm not going to bad cop the witness," Jack said, frowning and tapping her finger on the arm of the chair. "I'm Jack Duarte."

Daniel looked at the half-drunk bottle of sports water in his hand. "No, I'm good. Um. I already gave my statement and I'm pretty sure they recorded it. Do you have any leads? I'd really like to talk to my mother and check she's okay."

"We won't keep you long," Jack said. "We have a few questions, and then Detective Gage here will give you a ride home."

"I will?" Piper blinked.

Daniel looked at Piper and nodded. "All right, go ahead."

"Is there anyone in your grandmother's life who might've wished her harm? Who held a grudge? Maybe from her working life before she retired?"

Daniel shook his head. "No, everyone loves her, she's... she's beloved. Every Christmas she makes batches of cookies and hands them out to her neighbours. She volunteers at the homeless dinners her church holds once a month."

"What church does she attend?" Jack asked, cutting in. Daniel's eyes widened, startled.

"Uh, the Anglican church, in Onehunga."

"Note the church down," Jack said, glancing at Piper. Piper nodded and scribbled some notes down on their pad.

"Before she retired?"

"You mean, did someone from the local council kidnap my grandmother?" Daniel shifted, crossing his legs and uncrossing them again.

"Are you aware of any enemies she might have made back then? Maybe someone she beat out for a nomination or something?" Jack sat back in the chair. "I know this all sounds really cop show, but we need to know if there's anyone we should be talking to."

"They were all good friends," Daniel said, shrugging. "The ones who are still alive, who she knew, they're friendly. They call each other every now and then. That's all."

Jack glanced at Piper again, and they bent their head, making more notes.

"Wonderful. And your parents? The rest of the family?"

"Uh, I guess my uncle doesn't get on so well with her. He was in prison for a while, and she never forgave him."

"His name?"

"Abel Armstrong. He's reformed, got off on appeal. He works at a public library, now. Out East, like Māngere or something.

He's pretty boring, to be honest. I don't see him." Daniel checked his phone and fired off a text with his thumb.

"Daniel, would you mind not texting right now?" Jack said. "We won't be much longer, I promise."

"Oh sorry, it wasn't anything, just an emoji." He showed them both the chat thread on his screen and that he'd sent a thumbs up emoji to someone called Joe, who had asked if he was okay.

"What was he in prison for? Uh, your uncle, I mean," Piper asked.

"No one talks about it," Daniel said. "But I get the feeling it was something really bad."

The sun moved off them, beginning to sink behind the horizon. Jack looked at the house and back at Daniel. She tried to give him a reassuring smile, but she suspected it came out rather tight. "Great. Piper will give you our numbers, so you can get in touch if you think of anything else which might help us. Have you got someone to stay with? I'd rather you not be alone."

"I'll go to my mother's place. Get my boyfriend to meet me there," he said.

"Do you have any questions for us?" Piper asked.

"I guess just, is it likely she'll turn up again?" Daniel looked from Piper to Jack, his face hopeful.

"We'll do everything we can to bring her back safely," Jack said. "And we'll keep you updated. We can't make any promises, though, you know that, right?"

Daniel nodded and stood up to go, his shoulders rounded.

5

Jack tapped away at her computer, writing up the salient points from the crime scene and the interview with Daniel. The word processor was running slowly. The templates they used for official reports weren't loading correctly, and the Wi-Fi was being patchy, again. The list of suspects and leads kept reformatting itself to the wrong margin.

"Damn this place," Jack muttered, leaning forward over her keyboard as if that would make it work more efficiently. If only she could do the paperwork from home on her own Wi-Fi! Or if she could use her own format instead of these awful templates designed by someone back in the nineties.

Piper walked in and Jack looked up, relieved to be distracted from the paperwork.

"Did Daniel say anything new on the drive home?"

"Talked about his boyfriend, mostly," Piper said. "It was kind of sweet."

Jack smiled, it was nice that the kid had been so comfortable with them. To be out like that. When Jack was a teenager, people used lesbian as an insult. Piper was smiling, too, probably thinking much the same thing. *Say whatever you want about the queer scene,* Jack thought, *but we can do solidarity okay.*

"Nothing else?"

Piper shook their head. Jack sighed and looked back at the computer screen. "The uncle is the only lead we have."

"You really think a librarian could have taken her out of the house without anyone seeing anything and without opening the locked doors?" Piper tipped their head to the side.

"There was a spare key on the veranda, Daniel said he used it to get in. If he knew it was there it's likely others did too."

"Oh. Yeah." Piper sat in their chair beside Jack's desk and leaned on their elbow, resting their chin on their hand. "Well, how do we get more leads?"

"We have the church and the neighbours, lots of possibilities there. I'm sure someone saw something." Jack pulled out a printed map of the neighbourhood and circled the area with her finger.

"So, door knocking... and what happens if we don't find anything useful?"

"We might have to consult some specialists." Jack sniffed and sized Piper up. "You think you can handle talking to some witches?"

"Witches?" Piper grinned wide. "Hell yes."'

"Great." Jack nodded. "But the neighbours and church first. Which do you want to take?"

6

Piper spent hours door knocking. They'd been offered six cups of tea, and after the first, they'd turned them all down. Two doors had been slammed in their face and they'd had to knock again, show their badge, and convince people this really was an important conversation.

Maybe they should've asked a community constable to do this job? But hey, it beat chasing chickens, right? Or monitoring speeding cars?

No, they felt betrayed, or possibly disappointed, by the mention of witches. It was like Jack had waved the weirdest shit she dealt with in front of Piper's nose then taken it away again. At least it was a pleasant neighbourhood. One Tree Hill was right by Cornwall Park, an old English-style commons with stone walls and rolling green pastures. Sheep and cows grazed there, even. Piper liked the way the old English countryside blended into the modern suburban streets.

Moana Avenue itself was a wide street with centre islands green with grass. Trees were spotted at even intervals, shedding gentle shade on the road. There were a mix of shared units and big old villas, cats wandering about, and dogs eager to make new friends from behind their gates. There was even a little café where Piper took a break to eat lunch, sampling some of the homemade frittata out of the cabinet.

The neighbours mostly didn't seem to know Edith by name, only well enough to nod at her. Although, Mr Wolfgang – who lived in a modest ex-State house next to Edith's cottage – was particularly concerned. He invited Piper in and gave them a drink of water.

Jamie Sands

Jock Wolfgang was retired. He had a mostly bald head, with some grey hair remaining around the base of his skull, a scraggly beard which looked to be stained from nicotine, and a warm smile.

"I haven't seen her around. Usually I see her go to get the newspaper in the morning, but she didn't today. And if she was going away, she would've let me know to water her plants."

Piper bent their head and scribbled a note on their pad. "You're quite close to Edith, is that right?"

"I wouldn't say close," he said. "More like we're friendly as neighbours go. When she goes back home, I clear the mail, water the plants, check in a little bit. When I go visit my son in Wellington, she feeds my cat."

"Right, I see."

"And when we had that big storm last year I went around and checked she was all right. Half the suburb lost power that night, you know, and trees were down all over the place."

"I'm sure she appreciated having you check on her," Piper ventured.

Mr Wolfgang nodded, pleased. "She did. She was fine of course; very capable lady, that one." He frowned. "But... there's been police coming and going from her house, and if you're asking about her it's bad news, isn't it?"

"We're hoping not. We're just asking around in case anyone saw anything that might shed light on what happened." Piper shifted their weight from one foot to the other, feeling uncomfortable that this charming old man might think they suspected him.

"Let me know if I can help at all. She's a wonderful lady."

"If anything pops up that seems suspicious, you could let me know," Piper said, pulling out their card and handing it to him. He looked at it and nodded.

"I certainly will. Have you talked to the girl down the back?" His expression became disapproving as he shot a glance towards the next driveway. "I wouldn't be surprised if something had happened with her."

Piper sat up straighter, they hadn't expected such an interesting lead after the endless similar conversations.

"I'll head there next. Thanks for your help, sir."

"You can call me Jock," he said. "Miss... uh, sir?"

"Detective or Piper is fine," Piper said. The older folks were always a bit weirder about the non-binary thing, but Piper genuinely appreciated him trying to get it right.

Piper made their way to the house directly behind Edith's. From what Jock had said, they'd found a possible person of interest.

Piper knocked on a door which, unlike the others on the street, had a crudely painted pentagram on it. Witches?

Piper's heart sped up and they hoped very hard something cool and weird was about to happen.

After a moment, the door opened and a tall woman with striking purple-and-black hair looked down at them. She had several facial piercings: septum, eyebrow, and whatever you called the one in the upper cheek.

"Hello?"

"Hi, I'm Detective Gage. I'm making enquiries about a disappearance. What's your name?"

"Aeva du Maurier." Piper wrote it down.

Jamie Sands

"Hi, Aeva, I'm just asking around if anyone knows anything about Edith Armstrong, she's been missing since yesterday."

"I didn't realise being gone a couple of days was a crime," she said.

Piper gazed at her and tilted their head. They got the feeling they weren't about to be invited inside.

"It's not the being gone a couple of days, it's the manner in which she vanished." Piper swallowed. They didn't usually speak so formally; why were they trying to do it now? Were they trying to impress Aeva? Were they trying to be more Detective-like so that they could get out of this probation with a solid score and a permanent job? They'd better talk more normally.

"Vanished?" Aeva folded her arms.

"There were cookies burning in the oven and her grandson had heard from her an hour beforehand."

"Oh," Aeva raised her eyebrows. "Right, okay. Well, I dunno what to tell you, Detective. I wasn't home until late. I had a write-in at a café downtown and a bit of a big night afterwards."

"A write-in?" Piper scribbled on their notebook some more. They shifted their weight, trying to reduce the pressure on their feet, which were beginning to ache. Piper was beginning to feel awkward standing in the doorway.

"Yeah, a bunch of my writer friends and I sat in a café and wrote together. I write fiction."

"And then you had a big night?"

"With my Wiccan group. I can give you the numbers of the people I was with if you need an alibi?" She pulled out her phone.

"Yes, that'd be great. Is there any reason you... I mean, did you get on all right with Edith?"

"I wouldn't say we were friends," Aeva said. "I've brought home a few people over the last... year and a half since I've been living here and Edith made it pretty clear she didn't approve. She'd say shit about me being a woman living alone but entertaining different people, implying I was running a brothel or something, for goddess's sake."

"I guess, it can be hard with the older generations..." They'd been trying to get Aeva on side a little – maybe mention how Jock wasn't sure what to call Piper before – but Aeva interrupted, scowling.

"Whatever. It was none of her business and I told her so. She wasn't too pleased. Took me off the Christmas cookie list." Aeva bared her teeth in a forced smile which looked like a grimace. "I was so sad."

"You didn't get cookies from her?" Piper was amazed that these people all knew each other in the first place. On the street they'd lived on back in Christchurch the neighbours certainly hadn't been friendly like this.

"Nope." Aeva shrugged one shoulder. "We have different lifestyles, she couldn't handle a queer woman who worships differently to her living so close. Plus, I don't have a husband, so. I'm like, one of the nightmare witches her priests tell her are going to Hell. Stealing children and seducing men away from their wives, you know. All the old stories."

She rolled her eyes and seemed inclined to continue so Piper cleared their throat. "You know her grandson is gay?"

Aeva shook her head slightly. "I didn't know that. You want those numbers?"

"Yes. And what was the name of the place you met up at?"

Avea gave her the name of a café downtown and a friend who had hosted the Wiccan ceremony, and Piper left the house feeling they'd found a decent lead, depending on the alibi. They texted Jack and went back to the neighbourhood

café to have a coffee.

7

Jack crossed the entrance of the church, wondering if she'd be struck by lightning or maybe a booming voice would forbid her entry. Or her skin would tingle, at the very least. As it was, there was nothing, not the slightest frisson. Disappointing.

The church was empty but for a little old lady praying in the front pew and a middle-aged man talking to the reverend. Father? Vicar? Whatever he should be called. Jack strode up the aisle towards him.

It was a very pretty old church, rich with carved wood. The afternoon light filtered in through the high stained-glass windows. Unlike the last church Jack had been in, it didn't smell of damp or mould. In fact, it had a pleasant, cedarwood sort of scent, not too dusty, either. The pews looked worn but well cared for, gleaming with polish.

Jamie Sands

The priest saw her coming and patted the man he was speaking to on the shoulder.

"Thanks, I'll see you tomorrow."

"Good afternoon, Eddy, thanks for your help." The man nodded and passed Jack in the aisle as he left the church. The aisle was just wide enough that he didn't brush against her.

"Afternoon...Vicar?" Jack ventured.

"It's reverend in this church. Reverend Zebedee. And you are?" He reached for her hand. Zebedee was past sixty at a guess, his hair mostly grey. He was white, with a weathered face that indicated he had spent a lot of time outside in the sun. He had small, rounded, wire-framed glasses on and a warm smile.

"Detective Jack Duarte," Jack smiled politely and shook his hand. "I'm here about Edith Armstrong."

"Welcome to my church. Why don't we go into my office?" The reverend nodded at the woman praying, then led Jack to the front of the church and off to the vestry on the side. It was small but neat, with a little desk – two chairs on the guest side, one on the reverend's side. There was a window looking out onto a green garden.

"Please, take a seat, Officer."

"Thanks. It's Detective." Jack sat and shifted, uncertain what to do with her hands all of a sudden. The reverend smiled at her.

"Detective, sorry. Edith hasn't been into the church in several days. I had wondered if she was sick. I was thinking of dropping in on her this afternoon to check up. Now you're here I'm more concerned, I hope nothing has happened to her."

"We're not really sure what's happened. Do you mind if I record our conversation?" Jack pulled out her phone and pointed at the recording app.

"Not at all. Although it seems unusual."

"It's not admissible in court or anything, it's just for my record. I like to listen back later and see if there's clues I've missed."

Zebedee nodded, shifting in his seat to get more comfortable and folding his hands over his stomach. "Go ahead."

"Thanks," Jack said. She set the recorder going, placing the phone on the desk between them. "You said you had planned on dropping in on her. Do you do that often?"

"Once a month or so, maybe. Edith is a big help to me in the church; she's always on the board to organise the annual fair and helps with fundraising. She ran a collection for the vestry roof last month, a floral arrangement competition. Wait, I can show you."

He pulled out a small stack of printed photos and pushed them across the table towards Jack. She flipped through them, floral arrangements, people smiling, Edith and the reverend.

"And, as far as you know, was there anyone who held a grudge against her? Maybe someone who wanted to be the better fundraiser, or who squabbled with her over a pew?" Jack felt a little out of her depth with the specifics of church life, but she'd seen enough hobby related dramas to know it was likely.

The reverend tipped his head, trying to recall. "I'm sorry, but no. She's well liked. She teaches Sunday school sometimes. She invites me to dinner on Christmas Day. The kids love her."

"Are there any kids in particular, or any parents she's close to? It could be another lead."

He shook his head. "No, I think there's no one closer to her in particular. I can give you some names, though, if you need to talk to more people."

"Please," Jack said. "I can get a warrant issued to formally request those names and send it through. I know you'll value your congregation's privacy."

"Absolutely. I don't even let the kids take selfies inside the church," Zebedee said, chuckling a little.

"That's an unusual rule."

"Ah, it keeps their minds on the word of the Lord, not on the best lighting or the prettiest stained-glass window." He smiled fondly. "It keeps them a little more focused."

"I understand. Thanks for your help. I'll send through the warrant when I'm back at the station."

Jack's phone buzzed on the table and she picked it up. It was a text from Marlo. She dismissed the notification without reading it. Zebedee gazed out the window while she did, giving her some privacy. He took a breath and turned back to her.

"There was some trouble with her family some years back," the reverend said. "But as far as I know, it's all been resolved."

"You're referring to her son, Abel? Going to prison?"

"Right. Nasty business. Someone died – I'm sure you've read the files. She doesn't talk about it much. I understand he attends a church over in Māngere I think. And there was the sister, of course."

"The sister? You mean Camille?" Jack asked.

Jamie Sands

Zebedee shook his head sadly. "The other sister, Myrtle. Younger than Camille. She committed suicide after the court trial. Edith wasn't ever the same after that."

"Thank you, Reverend." Jack switched the recording off and stood up. "I'll leave you my card in case you need to get in touch. Anything you can think of, anything at all, would help."

"I'll call if I think of anything. Please, feel free to stay and worship if you wish to, or come back on Sunday for our service." He stood up from the desk and gave her a warm, almost paternal look.

"Thanks," Jack said, giving him another tight smile. There was zero chance of her coming back for the service on Sunday, and she was relatively sure Zebedee knew that, too. She texted Piper before she left the church.

I'm done, you?

Ready for pick up if you can come get me? :3

Jack got into the car and watched in the rear view mirror as the reverend left the church and walked down the side of the building. He didn't look furtive, exactly. But it didn't seem entirely normal, either. He was holding something she couldn't immediately identify down by his side.

Jack's heart started to thump and her eyebrows drew together. What could the reverend possibly be doing? Jack swallowed, slid out of the car, and followed him.

He went around the back of the church. She moved quickly but quietly to look around the wall. Zebedee opened a gate in an old fence. The wood looked weathered but sturdy.

He hesitated, looking up at the sky for a moment, before he crouched down, leaning on one knee. With two hands, he poured milk out of a bottle and into a dish.

The dish sat on one of the flagstones of a path leading into what looked like a kitchen garden filled with herbs and vegetables. It looked like it'd been sitting there empty, like the bowl she left out for the orange cat at home.

Jack's cheeks flushed with heat – here, she'd been certain he was up to something. She turned on her heel as he finished pouring, striding quickly so he didn't come back around and see her lingering.

She opened the car door and flopped down inside, running a hand through her hair.

"Nice one, Jack," she said to herself under her breath. "Distrust the sweet old man. The sweet old priest, for fuck's sake, he was just feeding his cat."

She stopped mid-stroke, remembering Marlo's jibe about the gesture. She rubbed her hand over her face a couple of times and slipped on her sunglasses, feeling rattled. This job was really getting into her brain.

She fired up the car and headed back down the road to

collect Piper. Maybe they'd had better luck.

8

All their life, Piper had loved stories about magic and mysticism. Their childhood games had all involved witches, wizards, werewolves, and fairies – making their brother be the bad guy who needed to be defeated, or the prince who needed to be rescued.

Somewhere along the way, the desire to defeat evil had translated into training with the police, and becoming a detective – it was a way to make a difference in the world, bring the bad guys to justice. But a large part of Piper still longed for magic and adventure.

That was their main motivation for asking to be assigned to work with Jack. Jack's reputation for the weird had called to Piper like a siren song, entrancing them and drawing them in. And now, it was about to pay off.

The store was one of those kind of places Piper had always been interested in but never quite brave enough to enter. It was named The Full Moon it was right in the heart of Karangahape Road, and it had little hand-written signs in the window for discounts on crystals, times for meet-ups, and upcoming book launches.

Jack didn't seem fazed. She pushed the purple-painted door open and ignored the jingle of the brass bell. Piper followed close behind. The shop smelt like incense and dust. Dreamcatchers, geodes, and books were everywhere. There was a table covered in little bowls, filled with crystals of all sorts of colours. Behind the counter was a shelf display of actual crystal balls.

"Afternoon, Valerie," Jack said, smiling finally. It didn't look a hundred per cent comfortable on her face, like she was rusty at making this particular expression. It was almost endearing.

"Jack, how's our favourite spooky cop?" Valerie was gorgeous, with thick red-brown hair with a gentle wave in it, and a heavy piece of pounamu around her neck. Her smile was soft and wide, welcoming.

Piper wondered if there was history here, too. If there was, it was only pleasant. Jack actually chuckled at Valerie's greeting. If you compared the relaxed body language Jack was showing now with how she'd behaved around Marlo, it was like two different women. Marlo had made Jack into edges and elbows, all hard planes. With Valerie, she was softer.

"Well, I've been given a sidekick," Jack said. She nodded at Piper. Valerie and Jack were both staring, and their gazes had weight to them. Piper swallowed and gave a finger wave.

"Hi, I'm Piper Gage. My pronouns are they and them. I just transferred up from Christchurch."

Valerie's smile was toothy and beautiful. "Oh, you're adorable, sweetie. Don't let Jack get you too jaded or serious, all right?"

"They specifically asked to be partnered with me, I think." Jack glanced at Piper with a sort of shine in her eyes, and her mouth was tugging up a little. Was Jack actually happy that Piper had asked to be assigned to her? Was she proud?

"How flattering. What wonderful thing did you do to earn a partner?"

"I guess it is kind of flattering, and they've been doing well so far," Jack said, giving Piper a half smile. Piper smiled back at the both of them. They could deal with being called a sidekick if Jack was proud of them.

"Well, I'm guessing this isn't just a social call?" Valerie picked up a rag and rubbed it over the polished wood of the counter.

Jamie Sands

"We've got a case of someone who has vanished and there's not much in the way of leads. There was some weirdness in the house. Do you know anyone around who's, y'know… sensitive? Who could maybe do a reading on the place and see if there's anything we've missed?" Jack had lowered her voice a little, although they were the only ones in the shop, and no one could overhear her.

Valerie smiled and nodded, going to consult a paper calendar pinned to the wall behind the counter. It showed three months and it was drawn all over with different coloured pens, names, and dates written haphazardly. "Let's see, the guy you used last time is out of town."

"Damn. I liked Cameron," Jack said, obviously disappointed. "He was funny."

"Everyone likes Cameron." Valerie nodded. She ran a finger across the weeks, speaking to herself more than to Jack.

"Hmm. Nova's good but oh, she might be busy with some family stuff right now, I just had a flash of something. Tom's a great psychic but he kind of hates the police, so, maybe not him. Aeva's a possibility, although she's not so strong."

"Aeva? I talked to an Aeva earlier, she lives right behind Edith," Piper said. Jack looked at them.

"Did she have an alibi?"

"She said she was at a write-in with some friends and then a Wiccan thing."

Jack looked at Valerie. "Does she hang out here?"

Valerie shook her head. "No, she's in a private group. They mostly keep to themselves, but she came by and signed up with me to stretch herself a little. I've not heard that she's very powerful."

Jamie Sands

"We'll check in on her alibi," Jack said. "Bit too much of a coincidence."

Valerie turned back to the calendar. "Or, oh, how about Emmaline? She's new to the city after a study break in Thailand. She's very powerful, very intuitive. I think you two – three –would get on very well."

"Thailand?" Piper said, impressed.

"Sounds fine, give her my number, will you? It hasn't changed. Like I said, missing person, weirdness. We have access to the house she disappeared from, if she needs it." Jack didn't sound impressed or excited.

"I got it, don't you worry. She'll be in touch soon, I'm sure." Valerie picked up a pen and pointed it at Piper. "Don't let Jack wear you down."

"Thanks, Val." Piper raised their eyebrows, surprised at the warmth in Jack's smile. Her expression was so often blank, or vaguely pissed off, so the rare expression held more weight.

Jack led the way out, Piper taking a final look at the shelves as they left. They probably didn't need a ceramic dragon. They didn't, right? Well, they could always come back later...

"That was so cool."

"Yeah, Val's awesome. Now, I reckon we need to get back to the station and compare notes," Jack said. "Then we check out Aeva."

9

"What about the parents?" Piper asked once they'd pulled away from the store.

"Whose parents?" Jack glanced at them and raised an eyebrow.

"Daniel's. Edith's son or daughter, and Daniel's parents. What have they said about all this?"

Jack frowned. "There wasn't anything in the file. Good catch. We'll have to look into it."

Piper breathed out, relaxing a little. Jack had said good things about Piper's work so far, and now she'd said 'good catch'. They'd be off probation soon if they kept up this level of work. Although, it did seem like Jack was a little distracted. Piper wasn't sure what it was distracting her, but they were happy if it meant they could be useful and remind her of things.

At the station, Jack and Piper collated their information and made up a list of suspects, putting files together for each of them. It was dull work, although Piper still felt a thrill of excitement every time they looked over to see Jack working away beside them. For all she'd complained about having Piper as a partner, she was perfectly willing to make use of them.

"What did you think of Jock Wolfgang?" Jack asked.

"I think he is a guy who loves his neighbourhood and has a bit of a crush on Edith," Piper said.

"What was your gut feel when you spoke to him, though. Anything suspicious?"

Jamie Sands

"Not at all," Piper said. "Which now that I think of it, seems suspicious. I should've asked to search his house. Why didn't I? What if he's got her in the basement or something?"

"We have no reason to suspect him, and 'he seemed too nice' won't get us a warrant, either. Sometimes a friendly neighbour is just a friendly neighbour. If you didn't get a weird gut feel about him, we can probably hold off on getting a warrant to search his basement."

Piper took a deep breath and mentally replayed the conversation with Jock before replying.

"No, I didn't get a weird feeling. He seemed really nice."

"Okay, so we'll put him down as a source of information but not a suspect at this stage."

Jack made sure Piper was watching and showed them the steps for how to enter the information correctly in the system. Piper watched carefully and made a couple of notes to refer to next time. The system wasn't intuitive, and their fingers itched to update it or make it more user-friendly, like they'd attempted to do at their last station. But that had been shot down, and Piper didn't want to push their luck here, as well.

Piper's head spun a little, so much new information, so many new things to remember and think about.

They couldn't wait to prove themselves – to Jack, to the sergeant, and to the station itself. But first, they needed a coffee.

10

Coleson walked in while Piper was in the staff kitchen, trying to understand how the coffee machine worked.

"Hey, new meat. How's things on the ghost beat?" Piper glanced up at him and gave him a tentative smile.

"No ghosts. I'm tracking a missing grandmother."

"Aw, see. That's too bad." Coleson moved closer. "I felt sure you'd have got the full Duarte conspiracy theory rant by now."

"Conspiracy theories haven't really come up," Piper said. They eyed Coleson and edged back from him.

"She hasn't mentioned that she thinks there're ghosts all around us, we just can't see them? That psychics and tabloid newspapers are all real?" He grinned wider, showing off his white, even teeth.

"We did go ask about a psychic," Piper admitted, before wishing they hadn't spoken. Damn needing to please people and be liked. They mentally kicked themself.

"Just wait, maybe get a beer or two in her, then she'll give you the whole rundown."

Piper tipped their chin up, determined not to be intimidated by him because he was tall, muscular, and white and they were short, rounded, and brown. He reached towards their hip and they flinched back.

"Sorry," he said. "Need a spoon." He pulled open the drawer they'd been partially blocking. Piper chuckled, but there was a weird vibe in the room. Coleson poured an instant soup mix into a cup.

Jamie Sands

"Why do you all make fun of her?" Piper asked, their mouth going slightly dry.

"It's teasing, jeez, can't you take a joke?" He flashed them a smile which should have been charming. It would have been charming – except this guy was a workplace bully. Piper had experience with these guys. Their heart sped up a little.

"Have you ever worked with her on a case?"

Coleson shook his head. "Me, nah. I stick to the vice stuff, you know. Drug busts, that kind of thing. Porn."

Piper pulled a face. They'd hoped Coleson at least had some experience working with Jack on which to base his opinions. "I'd much rather chase ghosts than bust kiddie porn rings."

"Ah, but someone has to shut them down, don't they?"

Piper nodded, someone had to shut those things down, but it didn't have to be them. It was good work, though, that he was doing. Maybe he was an insensitive jerk partially because

he had to put up walls to do his job?

Could be.

Or, Piper might be forgiving him too easily, too quickly. That

was also possible.

Sighing, they turned back to the coffee machine.

Coleson added boiling water to his cup and stirred it too fast,

slopping liquid out of the cup and onto the bench. He tossed

the spoon into the sink and picked up his cup. Piper eyed the

mess he'd made on the bench, but he ignored it.

"If you were smart," Coleson said. "You'd transfer right back

out of this place and find a mentor with a bit more clout. You

know, if you want to think about your career."

"My career?" Piper was about to add that their career was precisely zero of his business, but he ploughed on before they could say it.

"Right. You might be interested in all this spooky shit, but it's not exactly a path to the top. You want to impress the higher ups? You do it with arrests, with results. With rescued children and your picture in the paper. You do it by choosing a partner who people respect. Duarte might've been a cop for a while, but let me tell you something. Respect isn't a word people use around her."

"The sergeant seems to trust her," Piper mumbled.

"The sergeant gives her low-priority cases. Low importance. You think the world's gonna end if your missing grandma doesn't show up? People go missing all the time, and one grandma isn't going to make the papers."

"You're awfully concerned about the papers," Piper said, finishing up the cups of coffee she'd been making. "You been in them lately?"

"As a matter of fact, I have. Hey, if you're interested, you can come by my place and take a look at all the articles I've been in."

Piper turned and gave him a sceptical look. "You really think I'm going to fall for your line? Come over and look at my etchings? Seriously? You must think I was born yesterday."

Coleson smirked. "You don't get nothing if you don't try."

"Anything," Piper said, giving him a knowing smile all their own. He might think he knew everything about police work but they knew grammar. "You don't get anything."

They hurried out and down the hall to Jack.

"Hey Jack, you won't believe what this jerk said to me."

Jamie Sands

Jack looked up, bleary and tired looking. Her hair was a mess, partially standing on end from where she'd been running her hands through it. The top few buttons of her shirt were undone. Okay, well, she didn't look a hundred percent a respectable, professional police detective. If she were a guy, and a movie character, she'd have a five o'clock shadow and a cigarette hanging out of her mouth.

"Hmm?"

"Coleson. He told me all about how you're not a good mentor and no one takes you seriously, and then he had the nerve to ask me to his place. Prick."

Jack reached for a coffee cup. "Coleson's an asshole who's only looking to get ahead. He wants to make sure no one thinks anything good of me so he looks better by comparison. Ignore him."

Piper sat down and sipped on their own coffee. "I was going to."

"Wait. He asked you to his place?" Jack's nose crinkled. "I'll let the sergeant know he was inappropriate with you. Behaviour like that isn't acceptable.'

"I mean, I don't want to cause trouble when I'm still new to the department, to the station." Piper hedged, suddenly worried that it would work against their probation.

Maybe Coleson was right and they should have chosen an easier partner, someone who did run-of-the-mill cases with high solve rates. Something safe?

Jack fixed Piper with a look. "Don't do the thing where you make it — and yourself — small. He can't act that way. It's unprofessional and fucking creepy. I'll talk to the sergeant."

11

Jack didn't usually work such a long day, but she wanted to rule out Aeva if they could. Otherwise, this loose end would keep her awake. She looked Piper over and judged they could manage a couple more hours. She was feeling protective of them since the whole Coleson thing. Damnit, this enthusiastic newbie was really growing on her.

The café Aeva had named was on Karangahape Road, above a sex toy shop at the Ponsonby end. Jack led the way up the narrow staircase, trusting Piper to follow behind. Inside it was all patchouli incense, hand-painted Balinese flags, and old sofas draped with fringed shawls and scarves.

"This place is so great," Piper said.

"It's very... generic bohemian. Don't let on that we're cops," Jack said quietly. The café was quiet; a couple of people behind the counter, two people sitting half on top of each other and making out on a small corner couch, and a woman sitting at one of the few tables, writing in a notebook.

Jack approached the counter.

"Hey there, I heard about a writer's group that meets up here," Jack said, pitching her voice higher than usual. "My friend and I might be interested in joining." She gave what she hoped was a bright smile and nodded at Piper.

The man behind the counter's eyes were only half open and rather red, but Jack tried to ignore that for now. Not why they were there.

"Sure, we have a couple of groups that meet up, what kind of thing were you looking for?" He drawled, with a hint of an English accent.

"Oh, just something where people won't like, judge us for being queer or anything," Piper said.

Jamie Sands

"None of our groups would do anything like that," the guy said. He sounded a little offended that they thought it could be a concern.

Jack remembered Edith had gone missing on Tuesday. "I guess I have some free time on a Tuesday," Jack said, as if just thinking of it. "Do any of your groups meet up then?"

"I think one does, yeah."

The woman behind the counter, with line and watercolour tattoos of Disney characters up her arms, put her phone down and pulled out a clipboard.

"The sign-up sheets are all here." She set the clipboard down in front of Jack and flipped the pages until she reached one which read 'Tuesday' up the top. "The Tuesday group is pretty cool. You'll really vibe with them." She gave Jack an encouraging smile.

Jack grinned, seeing the sheet. It looked like it had never been changed. It had a list of names filling a third of the page.

"Awesome, do you have a pen?" The guy and the girl looked at each other and started searching for a pen. You'd have thought they'd have one handy for orders. Jack leaned in to scan the list. Yup, there was Aeva's name, fourth from the top, her handwriting large and loopy.

"Here," the girl said. She handed Jack a slightly chewed on ballpoint pen.

Jack wrote 'Jacky Pendalton' in the first free slot, but put her real phone number beside it, then handed the pen to Piper, who bent over the paper.

"Do all of them turn up every week?" she asked.

The guy laughed. "Ah, no; not all of them are here every week. Let's see, probably three turn up almost every time and the others are more like, they come and go."

It was gonna be a push to make this sound natural but Jack had to get the exact information.

"I don't want to join a group with only three people in it. Can you tell me which ones of them were here last week?" She pointed at the list.

Luckily they didn't seem suspicious, which was unusual. Unless? Yes, they were both high, weren't they? Jack was glad it hadn't made either of them paranoid.

The guy leaned in. "Oh man, so last Tuesday? Yeah, Yeven was there, Aeva, and Beau. Astra, George, and I think Nikau came for a bit of it."

Jack nodded and straightened back up, giving them a big smile. "Okay, that seems like a good turnout. Thanks so much, I guess we'll be back on Tuesday."

They both smiled at her. "You want a coffee or something?" The girl asked.

"Nah, I'm good, thanks, though. C'mon," Jack turned and led the way back to the stairs.

Once they were back on the street, Piper beamed at Jack.

"That was so cool! Fake names, pretending we were writers, I love it!"

Jack chuckled. "I sorta got the feeling if we'd told them we were cops we would've got far less information out of them."

"Do you trust his word that Aeva really was there last Tuesday?"

Jack tipped her head one way then the other and pressed her lips together. "For now, it's enough. I'd like to call one of the other people he mentioned." She pulled out her phone and dialled the number she'd been reciting in her head since reading it on the counter.

"Did you... Did you just memorise a phone number?" Jack held up a hand to quiet Piper.

Down the line, the phone rang two times before someone picked up.

"Hello?"

"Yes, hello is that Yeven?" Jack asked.

"Yeah, that's me."

"My name's Detective Jack Duarte, I have a couple of questions for you about last Tuesday."

"Last Tuesday?" The man sounded deeply confused, but he hadn't hung up, at least.

"Yes, did you attend a writing group at the Mistral Café?"

"Yes, ma'am, I did." His manner became a lot more formal, perhaps responding to her straightforward question.

"What time was that, do you remember?"

"Uh, I guess I got there at about two in the afternoon, and I was there a few hours. So probably until six or so."

"From two 'til six?" Jack asked, making sure that Piper was getting both sides of the conversation.

"That's right, ma'am."

"That's great, thank you. Can you tell me if Aeva du Maurier was there with you?"

"Yes, ma'am, she was."

"She was. For the whole time? Two until six?"

"Yes, ma'am. I remember because she sat opposite me." The man sounded more comfortable now, as if pleased he was being helpful, maybe?

"Thank you very much, sir. I don't have any other questions."

"Uh, no worries. I hope she's not in any trouble."

"No, she isn't. I just needed to confirm her whereabouts. Thank you for your cooperation."

Jack pocketed her phone and smiled at Piper. "Aeva's alibi is clear, she was here the whole time when Edith vanished."

"You're so badass."

Jack looked at Piper's expression, which was a complex blend of tired, hopeful, and uncertain. She may as well throw the kid a bone. "Come on, let's get you home. You've done good today, rookie." She led the way back to the car.

12

The next morning Piper woke up to the sound of thumping.

They blinked awake, peering at the clock beside their bed.

Six a.m.

Piper groaned, tried to bury themself in their pillow and go back to sleep, but the knocking at the door started up again.

They hauled ass out of bed and pulled on their fuzzy Wonder Woman bathrobe, shuffled to the door, and looked through the peephole. Jack stood there, hair pulled back into the world's tiniest ponytail, a tiny tuft at the back of her head. She looked impatient.

How had she got into the apartment building and up here?

Piper opened the door. "Jack?"

"Morning! I've been texting and calling, but you didn't reply. Emmaline got in touch, she wants to meet up now."

"Now?" Piper asked faintly. "It's six in the morning. You woke me up. You're at my house." Piper's brain processed slowly, trying to understand.

"Yes."

"How did you know where I live?"

"It's on your file. Are you going to invite me in? Your corridor is kind of on the cold side."

"Right, sorry." Piper stepped back and opened the door. "Come on in." As soon as they said it they realised the place wasn't that tidy. It wasn't dirty exactly, but it was on the messy side.

Jack moved past them and looked around the modestly sized apartment. "I'll make coffee while you get ready. Do you shower in the morning or evening?"

"The morning. Right, yes, I'll shower." Piper cleared their throat and hurried to the bathroom. "I won't be long."

Jack moved into the kitchen.

"The coffee and stuff is over the sink on the shelf, and the mugs are–"

"I'll find things. Go on."

Piper huffed out their breath and closed the door behind them, reaching to switch on the shower before disrobing. Their heart was racing from the wake up, and from feeling off footed.

How were they meant to know Jack was an early riser? Or that she'd want to meet this psychic or whatever she was first thing in the morning? Why not reschedule?

Piper didn't typically spend a long time in the shower, but this was a record. Lather, rinse, splash face, facial cleanser, rinse, get out. They hadn't brought any clothes in with them. They'd have to go through the lounge in their bathrobe. If Jack was concerned, she could've offered to wait in the car.

Mostly dry, Piper put their robe on and hurried to their bedroom, en route they glanced over to see Jack stacking and rinsing dishes. "You really don't have to do that!"

Piper slammed the door of their bedroom and had a momentary panic about what to wear. Should they dress like they had yesterday in a button-down shirt and slacks? Or shake things up in a dress? Or go casual with T-shirt and nice jeans? What had Jack been wearing? Had it been the same white shirt and black pants as yesterday? Lots of people at

the station had been in buttoned shirts... they wanted to

make a good impression. Maybe a shirt and skirt?

With a groan of annoyance at themselves, Piper pulled on a

flared dark blue skirt and a soft, loose blouse, tying a short

tie and settling it in the collar of the shirt.

There. It was hard to make skirts look gender ambivalent,

but Piper still liked to wear them.

Finally, they ran a comb through their hair, set it down and

pushed their hands through with a little product to

accentuate their natural tight curls. They nodded at

themselves in the mirror and went out into the lounge.

Jack had washed all the dishes Piper had been putting off for

the last few days and they were drying, sparkling, on the

dish-rack. The kettle was steaming and there were two cups

of coffee waiting on the table. The toaster popped and Jack

stacked the slices on a plate before offering them to Piper.

"You don't have any jam or anything, do you usually have it

dry?"

"Peanut butter," Piper said. They reached into the pantry and

brought out the jar. "You really didn't need to do my dishes."

"It's no trouble," Jack said. "I was waiting for you and figured

I might as well be useful. Bring it with you and we'll head to

the car." She moved towards the door.

"My god." Piper spread peanut butter on the toast and picked

them both up in one hand, grabbing the mug and swigging

from it. "You surprised me. I mean, yesterday was great, and

I learnt stuff, but I did not expect you to be a neat freak."

"Well," Jack said, her tone conversational. "My father was in

the army, and I guess we always had to keep things neat at

home. Besides, a cluttered house can lead to a cluttered

mind." She paused and turned to look back at Piper. "Shit, I probably crossed a ton of boundaries, didn't I? Coming here, doing your dishes. Look, it's been a long time since I had a partner I trusted. I overstepped, and I'm sorry. I didn't mean to. Shit, I should go. I'm so sorry." Jack turned towards the door.

"No, it's – it's fine, I'm up now, I'll go with you," Piper said. "It was just a very abrupt... morning. Yeah, you barged into my house pre-alarm and did housework. Maybe we need to talk about boundaries a little."

Jack moved to the table and sat down. "Boundaries are good."

Piper joined her and took a moment, examining the source of their discomfort. "Okay, so, I don't mind you coming around early, I guess, but you probably shouldn't do my housework. That makes me uncomfortable."

"Noted," Jack said, nodding once. "So, I'm sorry, I didn't mean to be insensitive. I just wanted to get going on the case, I guess."

"Thank you," Piper said. They felt a little of their discomfort drain away. "I'll try and remember to take my phone off silent so I can hear it if you try and get in touch."

"That sounds good."

They set their coffee cup down and stacked the toast on top so they could pull on their jacket. "I guess we can get going, then."

They both stood up and on the way to the door, Piper picked up their ring and slipped it on.

"May I ask about the ring?" Jack asked, looking at Piper's hand. "You were wearing it yesterday, but you leave it by the door."

"My grandmother's ring," Piper said. "When she died she left it to me and I've used it as a sort of good luck charm ever since."

"Nice." Jack pulled the door open and led the way out, hesitating for a moment in the doorway. "You're going to clean those dishes when you get home tonight, aren't you?"

"Yes, ma'am," Piper said. They hurried down the stairs, coffee slopping over the edge of the mug. Piper hissed as the hot liquid burned their hand, and they sipped some to stop it from happening again. The toast left a trail of crumbs, Hansel and Gretel style.

So much for cleanliness, they thought.

Once they were in the car, Jack didn't talk much; they didn't even play the radio.

Piper watched as the streets of Mt Albert passed by. They liked looking at the mishmash of early settler's homes,

Victorian-style houses, and new townhouses. It was always busy around here, too, which they liked.

Jack was glancing at Piper every now and then but mostly paying attention to the road, taking Dominion Road into town. Piper got the feeling she was making mental notes and filing them away in her internal 'Piper' record.

Piper felt a sudden surge of affection for this strange, skinny, white detective. She'd turned up out of nowhere, sure, but she'd realised the error of her ways and been almost sweet since.

Piper cleared their throat to ensure they weren't grinning goofily at their partner and breathed out shortly. "Right so, uh, Emmaline? She's a psychic, is she?"

"Right. The previous one Valerie set me up with was great. Cameron, he was charming, funny as hell, but he also helped me solve a particularly weird murder case."

"So, uh, being psychic is really real?" Piper made short work of the second slice of toast as Jack considered her words, staring at the road.

"Psychic seems to be, yes." Jack screwed her mouth up as they waited at a red light. "Now – don't get me wrong – those people on TV, reading minds and stuff? It's a lot of cold reading and careful use of psychology. But in my experience, some people know shit they shouldn't. Cameron had this way of looking into nothingness. And then, he'd have an answer. Sometimes he did a thing with a mirror as well, I can't really explain it."

"What else is real?"

The light changed and Jack drove through the intersection before replying, her voice careful and precise. "I know there's more out there. I've had this sensation of being at the edge of something. If I was on a beach I'd be where the water makes the sand damp, and my feet are getting wet when the waves wash in. Only, instead of it being the ocean, I don't know what it is. And I'm pretty sure the people involved are actively concealing the... not-an-ocean, from the rest of us. Does that make sense?"

"Perfect sense," Piper said, nodding.

"Because I could probably do a standing outside a locked door metaphor, too, if that would help." Jack glanced at Piper, her lips quirking up.

"It's okay," Piper chuckled.

They wondered if this was a version of the conspiracy theory rant Coleson had mentioned. They felt like they were getting the more honest version of whatever he'd heard, anyway. "Do you think ghosts are real?"

"It's an interesting one, and I have no idea if they're real or not. But it would be fun to find out, don't you think?" Jack glanced at Piper and flashed a smile which could have broken hearts. Piper nodded and smiled back.

"Definitely."

"And, well, Cameron and I found someone who can astral project."

"Astral... okay, remind me what that means?"

"When you can leave your body and your spirit goes somewhere without you. There was a little boy who kept doing it, really messed with his teacher. She thought her house was haunted or there was a poltergeist or something."

"Ohhhhh..." Piper finished their coffee and set their mug awkwardly in the car's cup holder, the handle didn't want to let it sit right. "Okay, that's pretty amazing."

Jack parked up in front of the Full Moon magic shop on K Road.

"It didn't suck," Jack said. "Well, once we'd worked out why the teacher's things kept turning up other places. Cameron wasn't a police officer. He just helped me out a couple times as a consultant. Emmaline will be the same. Come on, let's go meet her."

13

Jack had arranged to meet Emmaline at The Full Moon.

"It's not usually open this time of day, but Emmaline said she has a key or something." Jack said.

"Cool," Piper said. They could barely contain their excitement, palms sweating. Piper had been imagining all sorts of possibilities for what Emmaline could look like. Maybe she'd be a total Wiccan Goth like Aeva was? Maybe she'd be bald, wearing a white jumpsuit like something out of X-Men? Maybe she'd be in full Romani garb and ask them to cross her palm with silver? No. In fact, that was probably a super-racist thing to imagine. Piper scolded themself.

The door to the store opened and a short, white girl in her early twenties with long, wavy, blonde hair and big, bright-blue eyes waved at the two of them.

"You must be Jack?" The blonde said, with a hint of an accent Piper couldn't quite place.

"I'm Jack, you're Emmaline?" Jack and Emmaline shook hands, Emmaline looking up at her. Jack wasn't the tallest in the first place, but she was tall compared to this girl. It made Piper feel ungainly, way too tall and all elbows.

"C'est *moi*, and this is?" Emmaline turned to Piper and offered her hand.

"Piper," they said.

"My partner in this investigation," Jack added. "Piper uses they and them pronouns."

Emmaline smiled and shook Piper's hand. "It's a pleasure to meet you, too. Do you want to come in? I can make tea."

"I spilt half my coffee on the stairs," Piper said. "I'd love a tea."

"Sure," Jack nodded. "Sounds good."

Emmaline led them both into the magic shop and gestured for them to sit in an alcove where there were some battered old couches. Piper waited for Jack to sit and sat beside her. Emmaline brought a pretty tray of cups, a teapot, a sugar boat and a milk jug, and set it down on the coffee table, sitting on a couch at right angles to the one they were perched on.

"Valerie told me you need some psychic help," Emmaline said. She handed Jack a cup of tea. "Help yourself to sugar and milk."

Jack took a sugar cube and popped it into the cup. "We have a missing woman, Edith Armstrong. Taken from her house in a small time frame, and a note left behind mentioning a debt. So far we have a couple of possible suspects but we're not sure if any of them have a motive. And we have no idea where she is."

Emmaline sipped her tea while Piper added some sugar cubes and milk to their cup.

"Sounds straightforward enough. Do you have anything with you which belonged to her?"

"Not with us," Jack said. "But we have access to her house, which she vanished from. You can use anything you like there."

"Sounds perfect," Emmaline said, brightly. She gave Jack an appraising look.

"Have you done this a lot?" Piper asked.

"No, only a handful of times. I've been studying abroad for the last while, but I've helped on a missing child case in London once."

"How'd it work out?" Jack asked, rubbing her forefinger up and down the side of the teacup.

"We found her. She was out in the woods. It was... timely. She could have died of exposure if we'd been much later. The officer I worked with wasn't much of a believer, and he delayed on following my advice." She frowned, and Piper noted how her whole face changed when she wasn't smiling. She stopped sparkling.

"I asked for your help, it'd be stupid of me to ignore it," Jack said.

"Glad you think so," Emmaline's smile came back. "Call me Em, since I know Emmaline's a bit of a mouthful in English. Tell me about yourselves?"

"I don't really see what you need to know about us?" Jack said, glancing at Piper before turning back to Emmaline.

Jamie Sands

"I want to get to know you, it's nothing strange – I prefer to know who I'm working with."

"Boundaries," Piper said, feeling bold. Jack glanced at them and sighed a little.

"Sorry. Not much to know really. I'm an army brat, lived all over New Zealand growing up. I didn't want to go into the military myself but the police seemed a good option." She shrugged and looked at Piper.

"Oh, um, well. I'm from a blended family; my mum married my dad after his first wife died so I have a brother who looks nothing like me. But we're a close family, I came out as non-binary when I was fifteen and went to police college right out of high school. My mother died around then. I always wanted to do some good in the world and this was the best way to do it. I figured I'd do this for a while and eventually, maybe be a social worker or restudy to be a psychologist." Piper looked between the two of them. Emmaline smiled encouragingly.

"Go on."

"Well, I'd heard of Jack, of Detective Duarte, because she'd done some weird cases, and people talk. It sounded so interesting, so much more than the stuff I'd been doing which was a lot of lost cats, traffic control, and minor theft. I asked to be transferred and they approved it!"

"Is it true? You do the weird stuff?" Emmaline asked Jack.

Jack sputtered into her teacup, flushing pink for a moment. "The cases? Yes. If cases are inexplicable then I get given them. Some of the others at the station call me spooky. Because of the X-Files."

"Spooky. So cute," Emmaline said.

"It's pretty embarrassing," Jack said. But she was laughing as she said it, looking Emmaline in the eyes.

"I think you'd make a fine Fox Mulder," Emmaline said, leaning forward a bit more.

Jack cleared her throat. "Right, well, maybe we ought to head to Edith's house so you can do your thing."

Emmaline took the cups back and stacked them on the tray with the air of a cat who'd got the cream. Had they been flirting? And had Jack failed to cope with it spectacularly?

Jack wasn't meeting Emmaline's eye or Piper's, she stood up and spent some time adjusting her shirt and ran both her hands through her hair. "How are you feeling Piper? You want to drive?"

"Absolutely," they held out their hand for the car keys. "You all right, Jack? You seem a little off."

"I'm fine," Jack said, heading for the door, car keys in hand.

Emmaline followed them out and locked the door to the shop.

Jack went around to the driver's side and unlocked the car.

"I thought I was driving?" Piper asked, trying to bite back a

smile.

"Oh," Jack blinked at them. "Right." She tossed the keys to

Piper and moved to the passenger side. Emmaline waited and

then climbed into the back of the car.

"What were you studying in Thailand?" Piper asked, catching

Emmaline's eyes in the rear view mirror as they reversed the

car and started the drive to Edith's house.

"I was at a monastery," Emmaline said. "I was learning off the

monks there. Meditation techniques, tuning into the cosmos,

and honing my psychic skills."

"And you mentioned London as well? You must travel a lot,"

Jack said.

"I've lived all over. Raised just south of Paris until we moved to London when I was eight. I studied in an American university. My eldest brother lives there, so I stayed with him. After that, I've travelled to study: Thailand, Italy, Scotland, and here."

"How did you get into this line of work?" Piper asked. "How did you know you were psychic?"

"I was born into it, runs in my family," Emmaline said. "My mother is a powerful w... psychic. My father, too. My oldest brother is talented. It's only my middle brother who is totally without the gift."

Had she been about to say witch?

Witches were a thing, and Jack and Piper were non-judgemental enough to visit a shop that catered to witches to find help on a case.

So, why would Emmaline shy away from saying it out loud?

Piper bit their lip and swallowed the question. It could wait

for now.

14

Jack led the way to Edith's bedroom; Emmaline followed with Piper behind her, feeling slightly nervous about this whole thing. It wasn't that Emmaline doubted her own talents, it was more around what she could show the two police detectives, and what she'd have to paper over.

"This is where the note was. The note's been taken into the station as evidence, but the bed hasn't been disturbed. The indent was there when the grandson came in," Jack said.

"Interesting," Emmaline murmured, and moved into the room. She looked around at the trinkets – could be something useful there – then made her way to the end of the bed to look at where the note had been.

"Is there anything you need?" Jack asked. Emmaline looked up, met Jack's eyes – so warm and inscrutable – she shook her head.

"Only one thing. Be quiet, if you don't mind too much. I'll try and see..." She picked up a small book from the bedside table. A bible; an old and much-loved, red, bound edition with worn corners. *Perfect.*

Emmaline placed it on the palm of her hand and used the other to trace symbols on it with her fingertips. She started to sing, her voice a little softer than normal, vibrato giving away a little of her nervousness.

She was very aware of Jack watching her closely, Piper as well, but she was more aware of Jack. That woman had a presence.

There were little lights dancing around her hands, she hoped it wasn't too obvious in the daylight but, well, too late now.

Emmaline finished the song and the lights vanished. She frowned. That hadn't worked the way she'd wanted it to, and the remaining trace of magic in the room left a bad taste.

"There's something wrong," she said. Emmaline turned towards Jack. She opened her mouth and then closed it again, as if she was struggling to find the right words.

"Go on, what is it?" Jack said.

"It's..." Emmaline bit her lip before continuing. "Outside forces were involved here. I think I need to–" She looked away and frowned at the crease in the bedclothes.

"Outside forces?" Piper asked.

"I mean, this is going to take a little more time," Emmaline said. "Perhaps if you could give me a moment alone?"

Jack and Piper exchanged glances and Jack folded her arms. Emmaline got the feeling they weren't going to give her a moment.

Mon dieu, how should I handle this?

"Maybe you could talk us through what you're sensing?" Jack said, a little slowly. Emmaline might have lost Jack's trust – if she ever had it to begin with.

She chewed her lip and considered. These two needed to find the old lady, and Emmaline wanted that, too. She couldn't pretend that there was nothing more she could do. Helping this lost soul was far too important for that.

They dealt with the weird cases, they'd said. Well, she'd have to see how they handled the truth.

"The fact is, there are traces of magic here. I think she was taken by something... else."

Something else. Those words seemed to hang in the air between them and Jack's mind took a moment to process them. Emmaline was bullshitting her, right? Had to be.

"Something else? You mean like an animal?" Piper asked.

"No, like a sentient being. Something magical, but not human." Emmaline sat back on her heels and ran a hand through her hair. "I'm sorry, I wasn't sure how else to explain."

"Not human?" Jack asked.

Emmaline sighed, seeming to battle with herself before continuing.

"There's a trace of...Well, it doesn't seem as if it's..." she trailed off and then nodded. "It might be the fey. It could be them, in which case I'll need help from my brother."

There was a silence. Fey meant fairies, right? Like Tinkerbell. Like Peter Pan. She couldn't be serious. Cameron never pulled shit like this.

Jack felt her temper rise.

"You'll need to give us more details about what you mean, I think." Jack said.

"Piper, maybe you could put on the kettle for a cup of tea?" Emmaline said, turning her wide blue eyes to Piper.

"No tea, we just had tea. How about you tell us what you mean by fey?" Jack said, through gritted teeth.

"I'm not a psychic. I'm a magician, um... a mage." Emmaline got up from the floor and sighed. "I know this sounds pretty unbelievable, but we're going to need magic to find this woman and I can't just dance around it the whole time."

"Magic?" Piper repeated, their voice faint.

"Yeah. My brother trained with a fairy."

Silence stretched out as Jack tried to understand what Emmaline was saying. Sure, Jack had asked her in because she wanted the help of a psychic, but now Emmaline was saying something so far out of the realm of the known. Either she was being honest or she wasn't, and Jack couldn't prove it either way. Little lights from the hands? They had special effects better than that at Disneyland.

"Now, the fey, they're what you think of as fairies, only they're more like fairies from the old stories than from Disney. Fairies who steal babies and ruin crops. It's not really my thing, but Raphael does talk about it all."

"What's your thing?" Jack asked, her mind racing with possibilities. If Emmaline did know real magic, it changed a lot about the world. It would mean – what would it mean?

Jack let her breath out noisily. Was this the edge of things she'd been feeling like she was tiptoeing around?

Her temples pounded, threatening a headache, and her heart was racing. She couldn't parse this right now. She swallowed down the old feelings of panic which threatened to overwhelm her and let her logical mind take over her mouth.

"Okay. So let's say for the sake of argument that fairies are real."

"I can prove it, if you'd like?" Emmaline said. Jack and Piper exchanged looks. Piper's face was tense, jaw clenched, eyebrows up. Clearly Piper was buying what Emmaline was saying and it was freaking them out.

Jamie Sands

Did Jack want proof? Of course she did. If Emmaline tried to show them a trick and it was fake then they'd learn something.

If they fell off the cliff of reality and found out magic was real... Well, then they'd have learnt a lot.

Jack took a deep breath, stood up straight, and pushed her shoulders back. She nodded.

"As long as it's nothing dangerous, yes, we'd like some proof." She very much hoped she didn't regret answering in that way.

"I'll need a mirror," Emmaline said. Jack looked around the room.

There was a mirror with a fine, carved-wood frame hanging near the door to the bedroom.

Emmaline approached it and raised a hand. She began to sing again, this time in French. Emmaline's singing voice was soft and sweet, pure. It was charming, like listening to a soprano in an opera. But much nicer than any opera Jack had ever listened to.

She placed a slightly glowing hand on the surface of the mirror. It flickered. Jack thought perhaps it'd just been a flash of light from outside, somehow...

Jack and Piper both moved closer behind Emmaline.

The surface of the glass flickered again and turned liquid. After a moment, a boy's face appeared. He was pale with large dark blue eyes and high cheekbones, messy dark hair, and a puzzled expression. "Emmaline?" The boy in the mirror said. The picture resolved into better clarity, like a skype call when the interference clears.

Jack's mind raced. Was there any way Emmaline could have faked this? Set up an iPad or something to project onto the mirror? Her hands were free, there wasn't any evidence she had technology on her. And she couldn't have come to the house before this, it was a crime scene.

Although, no one was guarding it anymore.

Maybe Jock Wolfgang would be able to tell Jack if he'd seen Emmaline around. She'd have to ask him.

But Emmaline had just been told about the case, and Jack didn't think Valerie knew which case Jack was working, so she wouldn't have told her in advance. She couldn't have known, right?

There was a boy in the mirror. With deep brown hair and glasses on. "Emmaline? Is that you?"

"Hi, Gerard," Emmaline said. "Sorry to bother you, but have you seen my brother around lately?"

"Raphael? I think he was here yesterday, maybe, with Amy; but I haven't seen him today. I just got in, mind. Big night."

He wasn't a boy, Jack realised, he was probably in his early twenties. But young looking. His voice was heavily accented like a BBC reader, high-class English. It didn't seem like a recording, it seemed like he was really there.

"I need his help. Or maybe yours. I think we have a woman who may've been kidnapped by your lot,' she said, sounding sheepish.

Gerard frowned, although he hadn't smiled at any point. "How long ago?"

"Three days," Jack said, moving in closer to stand beside Emmaline, she met his eyes. If this was pre-planned maybe her intervention would show up the trick. "Have you seen her?"

Jamie Sands

"There – there's a lot of people in my lot, as Emmaline so eloquently put it. I'd need more information before I could tell you anything." He shrugged one shoulder, met Jack's eyes, and generally acted like a real actual person. Jack's stomach turned over.

"There's a lot of people being kidnapped?" Piper asked, their voice faint.

Gerard cleared his throat. "A description?"

"I'll do you one better." Jack went out into the hallway and came back after a moment with a picture of Edith. She held it up to the mirror and there was silence as Gerard examined the photo.

"I don't recognise her immediately. But then, I wasn't exactly looking for her. I – I think there's another revel tonight. I could go and check around. But you're sure it's my lot? They don't really go around kidnapping people for no reason. Not any more."

"Not sure at all," Emmaline said, shaking her head. Jack noticed Emmaline's accent turned more English as she spoke to Gerard, instead of the mishmash blend it usually was. "I need Raphael to get a proper idea of what's happened here. This isn't my kind of thing. If you see him, can you please ask him to get in touch? And thanks, if you could look for her that'd be super useful."

"Of course." Gerard nodded, looking at the photo again briefly. He opened his mouth, shut it again, and then spoke. "You know, if she was taken by certain people from our court, she could already be dead."

Piper sucked in their breath. Emmaline shook her head. "No, I think I'd know if she were dead. I didn't... sense anything around that."

"All right. I'll do what I can. Where can I get in touch with you?"

"Hmm." Emmaline frowned. "I'll call you again from the place I'm staying, you can use the mirror there to get back in touch with me." She wiggled her fingers at him by way of a wave.

"Perfect. Nice to, uh… nice to not quite meet you all. Talk to you soon, Em." Gerard raised a hand and the mirror's surface rippled. It went flat and ordinary again, reflecting Emmaline and Jack.

Jack turned away from it and ran a hand through her hair. Her hand came away with several loose strands on it. Jack brushed them away. This was beyond bizarre. This was the real stuff. Or was it?

She turned back to the mirror and pulled it off the wall, examining the back of it. Nothing there, no wires, no hidden technology. Just a brown paper mirror backing held on with tape. She ran her fingers over it to be sure, and to reassure her speeding heart. There was nothing to find. She hung it back up.

"Are you all right?" Emmaline asked, her tone uncertain.

"I don't know what to do with this information," Jack said. "I mean, it's great your friend wants to help, but where was he?"

"And why was he English? And all nervous and stuttering?" Piper added.

"Where? well, it's sort of like another universe. Faerie is a step sideways from here. I've been there one time but Raphael, he's my brother, he goes there a lot. Gerard is English. He grew up near London, but he pretty much lives in Faerie now. He stutters because he's nervous, I guess. His human form is pretty... I mean, he was always shy."

"Human form?" Piper's hand went to their forehead.

Emmaline looked between Jack and Piper, her eyes wide. "You're freaking out, right? You're totally freaking. I could have handled this better. I'm so sorry, I've never done this before. Come on, I'll make you tea in the kitchen."

"No, it's fine, I'm not freaking out. And we shouldn't make tea at a crime scene," Jack said, reaching to put a hand on Emmaline's arm. "I'm going to need a couple minutes to process."

"I think I need to sit down," Piper said.

Emmaline was instantly at Piper's elbow, her hand supporting them. "Come on, into the kitchen. We can sit down, at least."

Jack crossed the room to take Piper's other elbow. "No passing out, Piper. You're safe, you're not in any danger. You don't need to pass out, just breathe in and out."

Emmaline and Jack half carried Piper into the lounge and sat them on the couch. Emmaline rushed to the kitchen and came back with a large glass of water. Jack rubbed Piper's back.

"Just take deep breaths, okay? Keep on breathing."

Piper heaved in some breaths, breathing in and then in again.

"Let them out as well, love," Emmaline said. Piper let out a loud breath.

"That's it, take the water, have a little drink," Jack said. Piper took the glass in a trembling hand and took some sips of water. "That's the way, much better."

"I know you said there was weird stuff, but I didn't know it'd be a zoom interview into another universe. Who was that guy? Does he do magic, too?"

"Not exactly." Emmaline sat in the armchair and tugged it closer to the couch.

"He grew up here. The human side of the mirror, but he's a changeling. Him and his twin sister. They're half fey, I mean, half fairy."

"One of their parents was a fairy?" Piper asked, wrapping both hands around the glass of water. Emmaline nodded.

"So fairies are real, and they can mate with humans, and there can be half humans, half fairies," Jack said, half to herself.

"This is so confusing," Piper said, and rubbed a hand over their eyes.

"He mentioned revels?" Jack dropped her hand to her lap and took a breath. "Is it a party?"

"Mm-hm, it's a big, raucous, dangerous party. The ones Gerard goes to, they're rough. Like, all sorts of stuff happening."

"Stuff?"

Emmaline hesitated, her nose crinkling up in a cute way. "You know, rough sex, kinky sex, shapeshifting, torture – so much sex."

The room was silent for a moment as Jack and Piper considered this, and Emmaline looked at her hands. Jack imagined bad fairies, stealing people and having kinky sex with them. She wondered...

"Sacrifices?" Jack asked.

"Yeah, I think so."

"Holy shit." Piper set the glass down on the table and leaned down to place their head between their legs.

Jack resumed rubbing Piper's back.

15

Jack dropped Emmaline back at the magic shop and gave her a business card.

"Call as soon as you hear anything. I think Piper needs to rest."

"I don't mind coming with you," Emmaline said. "You need to deal with this, process this, too. You can talk to me, I'll answer any questions you have."

"You said you'd be calling Gerard from a new mirror," Jack reminded her. "And he's going to get us the information we need."

"Oh, right." Emmaline nodded and pulled her hair into a twist on her left side. "I forgot. Sorry. I'll call."

Jack saw the gentle pink blush on her cheeks. It made her feel warm. Something in her softened. "And, hey, thanks for all this. I appreciate it."

"It's no trouble." Emmaline put a hand on the roof of the car and leaned down. Jack half smiled at her through the open window.

Piper shifted in the passenger seat, their face paler than their usual warm brown. They groaned softly. Jack nodded. "Well, better go. See you later."

Emmaline waved as they drove away.

After a few minutes, Piper sat up straighter.

"You, uh, like her, huh?" Piper asked, their face passive. Jack shot them a glance, and Piper blinked back at her.

"Hey, no. Don't go making assumptions. We met her this morning and she's helping us out in our investigation with her specialist abilities."

"Uh-huh. Cause she's hella into you. Anyone could see, I could see, she was watching you and offering you tea and she was, like, smiling and blushing and playing with her hair."

"She offered you tea, too."

"Still," Piper said. "It wasn't the same."

Jack shook her head. "Nope, this conversation isn't happening. So. Magic is real, and there's a world full of fairies who apparently regularly kidnap people."

Piper huffed and Jack breathed out loudly. Then she laughed at the sheer ridiculousness of what she'd just said. Piper glanced at her, and chuckled a little as well. They both laughed for a full minute. *Releasing the tension, Jack thought.*

"I don't even know how to adjust to this. My heart keeps racing. Maybe I'll read a bunch of fairy tales tonight." Piper leaned their forehead against the window and stared out at the city.

"It might actually help," Jack said. "But, like, give yourself some time to relax as well. Maybe have a bath or something."

It was probably saying too much, crossing a boundary, to suggest that, but she was relatively sure Piper'd had a panic attack back there. They were looking much better now, but Jack knew from experience that panic attacks took time to get through properly. Their body would need some down time, some time for the adrenaline to process through the bloodstream.

"Aw, it's like you care about me," Piper said, reaching over to pat Jack's arm. Jack glanced at Piper, maybe they'd gone a bit punch drunk in the wake of the panic. Jack was sure they wouldn't be speaking like this even a couple of hours ago.

"Please don't touch me," Jack said, but it rang hollow. She tried to channel Idris Elba's quiet cool.

"You're not as mean as you pretend to be."

"Okay, you get one more comment, then the car becomes a place of quiet contemplation," Jack said. Although, maybe she shouldn't have given them that. Even. How was Piper so insightful? Jack hadn't thought she was an open book.

Piper grinned and sat up straight, half turning to face Jack, straining the seatbelt over their shoulder.

"You care, and you think Em's cute, and she definitely thinks you're cute and you should totally ask her out and kiss her and have like a hundred of her babies."

Jack snorted. Piper let the car be silent after that, and Jack was thankful.

She dropped off Piper at her apartment building. "I'll call if there're any developments. Now, get out of here."

"Night, Jack," Piper said, and got out.

16

Driving off, Jack was finally alone with her thoughts. There was a pain growing behind her right eyebrow. What had Emmaline meant when she'd said there was another world sideways to this one?

Jack shook her head. It didn't matter. In fact, Emmaline doing magic didn't matter. The existence of magic users in the world wasn't something she needed to worry about right that second. The only thing she needed to do was solve her current case.

Their case, she mentally corrected herself. Hers and Piper's.

As she drove into her neighbourhood, she felt the pain behind her eyebrow fade a little. The familiar intersection between business park, tourist area, and family restaurants from all over the globe soothed her. She could generally let go of the intricacies of her job, forget the stresses as she made this drive.

Jack lived in Epsom, but not on one of the rich streets. She was in a two-level townhouse on a street back from the busy thoroughfare of Manukau Road. She drove past the rundown stores, a particularly good ramen shop, and an arthouse movie theatre before turning onto her street.

It wasn't exactly a fancy house but it had character. It matched Jack. Getting a bit old, a bit scruffy, but comfortable. There was a nice tree on the footpath outside.

Jack let herself into her house and locked the door behind her before heading upstairs to the main living area. The balcony door stood open, and she brought in the bowls she'd left out for the orange cat that sometimes came to visit. She rinsed them, filled one with fresh water and the other with cat biscuits, and put them back in the same spot.

Jamie Sands

She took a shower and changed into a soft plain grey T-shirt and track pants. She was in the kitchen making some pasta when the doorbell rang. A part of her wondered if it was Emmaline. A foolish, silly, hopeful, part which she tried to ignore.

She pulled the door open, took in the legs, and her heart sank.

Marlo stood on the footpath, striking as ever.

"I wasn't sure if you'd open the door to me," Marlo said. Her hair fell in soft waves about her face, framing it perfectly. Jack's heart swelled with the old feelings. Affection, hope, and a little fear.

"If I'd checked I might not have."

"You're still funny. May I come in?"

"It's not a great time."

"You're just out of the shower, I can see from your hair. Which probably means you're making yourself a sad pasta dinner. Let me in, I'll make your sauce tastier." She breezed in past Jack. Marlo could always render her speechless.

She locked the door behind her – A cop could never be too careful – and followed her up the stairs to the kitchen.

"You don't need to do that," Jack said.

"It's not a problem. I worry about you, you know. Always eating the same thing, never relaxing," Marlo said.

"I don't eat the same thing all the time, and I didn't invite you in," Jack mumbled.

Marlo swept into the kitchen, snatched up a wooden spoon, and started fussing with the sauce on the hob. "So, what've you been working on?"

"You know what I've been working on, you saw me at the house." Jack hovered, unsure what to do in the kitchen with Marlo taking over.

"I'm interested, is all. Making small talk." She eyed the spice rack and pulled down the little container of dried basil, shook some into the pan, and stirred it in.

"Missing persons case, you know the circumstances. Marlo, seriously, what are you doing here? You didn't call, you didn't warn me you were coming, and you said when we last spoke you didn't want to be part of my life anymore." Jack folded her arms and glared.

Marlo shrugged, leaned in, and brought the wooden spoon from the sauce up to her lips. She made an orgasmic noise specifically designed to drive Jack crazy before taking the pasta off the heat and draining it.

"I've missed you. I know I said some stuff, I know I—"

"Broke up with me in a spectacular screaming tantrum?" Jack finished for her. Marlo didn't reply for a moment.

"Well," she said, after a moment's silence. "I'm human, aren't I? I can make mistakes."

Jack blew the air out of her lungs and went to get two shallow bowls to serve the pasta in. She averted her eyes from Marlo to try to think clearly. She laid the bowls beside the stovetop.

"Sure, you can make mistakes."

"I want to be in your life, Jack. Is it so wrong of me? I miss you."

"No, you miss the idea of me," Jack mumbled.

Marlo's head twitched. She'd heard. She didn't respond.

When the pasta was dished up they moved together to sit at the kitchen table, for all the world like it was a few months before and they were still together. Jack watched Marlo and stewed.

I could offer her a glass of wine, Jack thought, *but I don't want to. She doesn't deserve wine.* Besides, there was every chance Jack didn't have a bottle of wine to offer. She hadn't been to the supermarket in a while.

"This is lovely," Marlo said, smiling in the most fetching way. Jack was sure it was a smile Marlo practised in the mirror. "I miss these evenings, staying in with you."

"Do you? What have you been doing with your time instead? It's been – what – three, four months?"

"Oh, this, that, and the other," Marlo said lightly. Her tone. The light 'you don't need to know any details' air to her reply. It was so familiar. The secret keeping; withholding information so that Jack never felt like she understood everything, so that Marlo could hold it over her.

All the old rage bubbled up.

"Great, sounds interesting." Jack ate quickly although her appetite had vanished. "Are you seeing anyone?"

Marlo blinked, her eyelashes fluttering. She hadn't expected that question. "No."

"That's a surprise. I heard you were having dinner with Arabella the day after we split up." Jack said, her tone crisp and expressionless.

"Arabella and I are only friends, darling, don't be jealous." Marlo dropped her voice to a seductive purr. "You know I'd have to punish you if you got jealous."

Jack flushed against her will, her mind serving up memories of some of the better times she'd spent with Marlo. Part of what had worked between them was the way they both enjoyed power exchanges.

Jamie Sands

Then she remembered Emmaline describing parties in Faerie and the way she'd said 'kinky sex'. It jarred Jack back into the present moment.

"We don't have that kind of relationship anymore, Marlo. Leave it." Marlo's foot gently rubbed against Jack's calf, tantalising.

"We could, though. I'd love to see you back on your knees."

Jack pulled her legs back under her chair, out of reach of even Marlo's long legs. Jack set her fork down and forced herself to look Marlo in the eyes.

"Stop it. I don't want it from you anymore. We split up, I don't think I have to remind you why, or that it was actually your idea in the first place. Are you done? Maybe you ought to be going."

"Bit rude, darling," Marlo said.

Jack stood, picking up the bowls even though there was still some food in them.

"I need an early night. Had a pre-dawn start today. I'd say it's been good to see you, but it hasn't, and you know I can't abide liars."

To her credit, Marlo stood up, using both hands to fluff out her long, wavy hair as she pouted. Jack tried to focus on the dishes and not on watching her.

"Wouldn't want to be in the way."

"You know the way out," Jack said shortly.

She turned to usher her out, anyway, half to make sure she actually left the building.

She closed the door behind Marlo, slid the bolt home, and the safety chain. Then she leaned her back against the door and took a deep breath.

Jamie Sands

I'm safe, she told herself. *I'm safe and nothing bad is going to happen to me.*

What a day. There was too much to process. Jack headed into the lounge and sat on the floor in the middle of it, crossing her legs and opening an app on her phone.

Meditation should clear her mind and calm her temper.

No. There was something even better she could do.

17

Piper woke up to their phone ringing.

Half awake, they turned over and grabbed the phone. Five thirty a.m. Jack calling.

"Hello?"

"Piper, Em's been in touch, she has information for us. Are you up?"

"No, why are you? Did you even sleep?"

Jack spoke fast. "I realised that since magic is a thing, a couple of my unsolved cases can be explained that way. David Andrews didn't die of a heart attack, but there was no way anyone could've gotten into his Parnell penthouse – he had too much security on the doors and there were cameras everywhere in the common areas. He was found in the bathroom, in front of the mirror."

There was an expectant pause. "And?" Piper asked, interested despite themself. They were aware that their voice was thick with sleep.

"And it could have been a mage or a fairy who came through the mirror and strangled him. I know the contusions on his neck meant something but there was no way to prove it. There's still no way to prove it, but at least I can close the case in my mind. Are you awake?"

"I was asleep, like all the sensible people."

"Uh-huh. I'll be at your place in five minutes." Jack hung up.

"Well, crap." Piper slid out of bed. No time for a shower; unless?

Piper took the fastest shower of their life, pulled on the first clean clothes at hand – a plain green v-neck T-shirt and jeans – and was in the process of locating their sneakers when there was a knock at the door.

"Piper?" Jack called. "Are you ready?"

"Coming, keep your shirt on." Piper grabbed their badge, wallet, keys, grandmother's ring, and opened the door, grabbing their stab vest and a white bomber jacket with huge blue flowers on it in case it was cold out. "Good morning. You're awful and I hate you."

"So, get a transfer back to your old station," Jack said. "No skin off my nose." She winked, turned, and led the way to the car.

"I need coffee. You need to go via Starbucks," Piper said. They felt a little stung by the transfer remark, especially after Jack had been so sweet to them last night when they'd panicked. Maybe something had happened that'd soured Jack's mood? Maybe it was just the early hour.

"You sure you don't want real coffee?" Jack asked. "There's a nice place on our way."

"No, I want a gigantic cup of Starbucks," Piper said. "For sure."

"Should we get something for Emmaline, too?" Jack asked. Piper grinned at Jack's oh-so-casual suggestion.

"Yes. I bet Emmaline likes pink unicorn fluff things or whatever cute Instagram drink is in fashion right now."

"Of course she would." Jack nodded and made the turn that would take them to the nearest Starbucks.

"Who's David Andrews?" Piper asked. The name had been in their head since Jack had called earlier. It sounded familiar.

"He was this stockbroker, real bastard, started as a banker and moved into the share-market. Lots of people hated him, but it was a genuine locked-room mystery, one of the few cases I wasn't able to close," Jack said. Her eyes looked a little wild. Piper wondered if she'd slept at all.

"So now you have an explanation, but you can't close the case? Doesn't that bug you?"

"It was three years ago; all the trails will have gone cold. And someone else is living in that penthouse now. It's okay. It's good to have an explanation, or a possible one, anyway."

Jack pulled the car up at Starbucks.

18

"Aren't we going to the magic shop?" Piper asked, balancing two large Starbucks cups and a bag of pastries. Jack was sipping from a plain but giant coffee in a black reusable cup. "She invited us to the place she's staying, I think she said it was a friend's place who's out of town."

"Are you sure she invited both of us?" Piper asked.

"Yes, shut up."

The drive over the harbour bridge was quiet, Piper sipping coffee and Jack grimly navigating the roads in the pre-dawn dimness. Emmaline's friend had a house in Devonport. They pulled up at an apartment building on a particularly pretty road leading down to the water. Jack checked her phone.

"Number 2104."

They climbed the stairs, knocked on the door, and Emmaline answered promptly.

"Oh my goddess, did you get Starbucks!?"

"This one's yours, we didn't know what you liked so Jack ordered you this. It has hazelnut syrup and cream and things," Piper said. She handed her the cup.

"Perfect, it smells wonderful." She wrapped her hands around the cup. "Come on in."

They entered the dining area of the apartment. It was furnished in a modern Scandinavian style, very sparse with greys and plain wood. It didn't seem like a place Emmaline would choose to live in. She invited them to sit at the generous blond wood table. Piper shared out the pastries and after a moment, Emmaline began speaking.

"Gerard got in touch. He went to the revel and the afterparty to try and talk to as many people as possible."

"Has it been long enough to go to two parties?" Piper asked, checking the time on their phone.

"Time moves differently over there. It's been hours longer," Emmaline said.

"Did he see Edith?" Jack asked, leaning forward on one elbow.

"No, he didn't. He said during the busy times of the revel he was mostly occupied. Blindfolded. But he asked his master and got the name of someone who apparently smuggles things into Faerie." Emmaline's tone had been ordinary, conversational, but the subject of it wasn't ordinary at all to Piper.

"His master, did you just say?" Piper asked.

"Mm-hm." Emmaline nodded. "He has a master, it's a dark fey bond thing. But all the sex and torture is consensual, Gerard is happy with the arrangement. Loves it, even."

Piper sat back in their chair, not at all sure how they felt about the idea of a consensual sexual master, especially if it came with torture.

No, they were sure; it made them uncomfortable.

"So, who's this person we can talk to?" Jack asked. Jack didn't seem concerned about any of the torture and master stuff. She calmly asked questions about the investigation.

"I don't know if they're a human, Gerard said he couldn't get many details. But their name is Melchizedek." Emmaline pushed a little piece of notebook paper towards Jack with the name written on it. Jack reached out to take it and they almost brushed their fingers together.

"Melchizedek? How do we find them?"

Emmaline hesitated. "Gerard didn't... exactly know. The fey aren't straightforward. But he said if there was a kidnapping or people who were being stolen into Faerie, he'd know about it, and he was probably who was doing it."

Jack sat back in the chair and tapped her fingers on the table. "I guess we need to ask around, then."

"I might know someone who'd know someone. My brother, if I can track him down. Gerard said he still hadn't seen him." Emmaline picked up a cherry pastry and nibbled the corner of it.

"Surely someone at the magic shop could help?" Jack asked.

"Maybe."

"Did he find anything else out? You said he was at two parties," Piper said. They started pulling strips off an apricot Danish.

"He said there were rumours of a kidnapping, slave trade, human trafficking ring. I don't know if there was any truth in it, but he said he'd investigate," Emmaline said.

"You mean this could be the latest in an ongoing thing? A bunch of other people could have been taken over there for kinky sex and parties, torture? Worse?" Jack pulled her notepad out and scribbled something Piper couldn't make out.

Emmaline shrugged and swallowed a bit of pastry before she answered. "I don't know, it's possible. They fey are into it all, traditionally. I mean, the dark fey anyway. They see sex and kink and pain as normal."

"Should we go over there and help him investigate?" Jack asked. Piper looked at her with wide eyes.

"I don't want to go to the kinky sex place," they blurted. They just couldn't help themselves, the idea of it was creeping them out.

Jamie Sands

Emmaline and Jack both turned to look at them. Which made their stomach turn over and their mouth dry out. Piper picked up their coffee and downed the dregs, it didn't make them feel much better.

"Are you okay?" Jack asked.

"Piper might be right, I don't think it's safe," Emmaline said. She tipped her head to the side and pursed her lips. "But I need to talk to my brother, anyway. Maybe there is a way. It feels like the best leads would be on that side. But until I hear from him, I don't know."

"Wait, what does 'on that side' mean?" Piper asked.

"That side of the mirror," Emmaline said. "In Faerie."

Jack's jaw worked, betraying the slightest bit of tension which showed Piper she wasn't actually taking all this in her stride. "All right, so in the meantime, we can talk to your person, ask around at the magic shop and, what, check if any of our suspects know about or in fact, are, fairies?"

"Right." Emmaline nodded and finished off her coffee. "Thanks, that was really yummy."

"Any time," Jack said. Piper looked between them. If they were flirting they were doing it very much on the downlow.

"Speaking of time," Piper said. They stifled a yawn. "I'd really like it if we could start meeting after seven in the morning. Or eight in the morning, even, I mean, it's usual business hours."

"Sorry, love," Emmaline said. Putting a hand over Piper's. "I'm jet lagged all to hell, time's become meaningless." Piper looked at Jack, who shrugged.

"I don't sleep much," Jack said. "Especially not when I have a case on the go."

"But I can totally just do other stuff until a reasonable hour," Emmaline said. She patted Piper's hand, which probably should have felt condescending but Piper trusted that Emmaline didn't mean it in that way.

Piper shuddered. "I hope we're done early enough tonight so I can get some beauty rest."

"Beauty sleep? Not compatible with the police force," Jack said.

"Ignore grumpy, you don't need beauty sleep, Piper. You're gorgeous already." Emmaline squeezed Piper's hand and then let go. Piper gave her a wide smile.

"Thanks, Em. Can I ditch Jack and be your partner instead?"

"No, trust me, it's boring being me. All right, so. Are we splitting up to talk to more people, or what?"

"No, I think it's best if we stick together. From what you've said fairies aren't exactly friendly, and we're safest as a group," Jack said. She'd scribbled a few more notes on her notepad.

"Right, I'll see if I can get in touch with my friend, then," Emmaline said.

"Piper, would you check in with the station and see if anything new has come in they might've forgotten to mention to me?"

"Will anyone be in this early?" Piper asked. They were already getting out their phone, but it was hard to imagine the station being busy this early in the morning.

"I'm sure there'll be someone there."

Piper nodded and went to make the call. Apparently, Emmaline was doing the same. Jack cleared up the reusable mugs and plates and presumably went to clean them up and polish every surface in the kitchen. She left the last pastry on a plate on the table.

Suzan, one of the junior officers, answered Piper's call. Piper was pretty sure Suzan was one of the ones who made ghost jokes about Jack on their first day. But they gritted their teeth and projected cheerfulness. "Hey, Suzan, it's Piper."

"Hi, Piper, you're up early."

"You, too! You pull an early shift?" Maybe Suzan was going to be nice to them, after all. Maybe they could make Suzan an ally in the station?

"Yeah, but I don't mind it too much. How can I help?"

"I wanted to check if there'd been any updates on the Armstrong case? Any calls or anything turn up since yesterday?"

"I think the parents are coming in today. Um, Edith's daughter and husband, Daniel's parents. Just a mo–" Piper heard a keyboard tapping, then Suzan made a pleased noise. "Yeah, they're coming in. If Jack wants to talk to them she'll need to be in around midday."

"Midday. Fantastic, thanks, Suzan."

"No worries, Piper." Suzan totally sounded friendly. Piper felt like they'd made some headway there, at least. Feeling a little warmer about the world, Piper hung up and went to find Jack who was, in fact, rinsing and stacking dishes in the dishwasher. They updated Jack on the news from Suzan and Jack nodded.

"Hopefully Emmaline can contact her friend and we'll have a full day of interviews."

Emmaline came in after a few minutes to find Piper wiping off the dishes with a tea towel. She shook her head in disbelief.

"Police in this country are so weird. My friend Deacon's free this morning. We can head over right now. If I could track Cameron down he'd be even more help, but it seems he's off on a honeymoon or something." She picked up the last pastry and took a big bite.

"Cameron, like, the psychic Cameron I worked with before?" Jack asked. She folded the tea towel neatly and hung it over a cupboard door.

"Uh-huh, he's not psychic, though. He's a mage like me. He and my brother studied under the same master," Emmaline said. She'd inhaled the pastry and was now dusting off her fingers.

"Master, the way Gerard has a master?" Piper asked. Their mind raced, trying to connect the dots. Did all fairies and humans end up in kinky relationships with power exchanges?

"No, their master is a free fey, not unseelie. And it's master as in teacher, not the other kind," Emmaline said.

"That's something. Shame, I would have liked to see Cameron again. Honeymoon, you say?" Jack asked.

"I don't know much, but Gerard mentioned his sister and Cameron being a thing," Emmaline said. "Gerard's sister Lina is super adorable. I can see them getting on really well."

"Right, so we should go and see Deacon?" Jack asked, pulling her car keys out of her pocket and jiggling them in her hand.

"He lives across town, Blockhouse Bay."

"All the way over there? At the start of rush hour?" Jack tossed the keys to Piper. "You drive."

19

Deacon lived in a long, pale-grey house split into several units. It sat on a leafy road on the crest of the hill, overlooking a rolling park on one side and the ocean on the other.

"This place is nice," Piper said. "I guess there's a lot of money in being a mage, huh?"

"Depends what type of mage, and what you do with it," Emmaline said from the back seat. She leaned forward. "Listen, don't try and arrest him, all right? He doesn't actually break the law, he bends it."

Jack half turned to fix Emmaline with a sceptical look. "What was that?"

"He won't give us information if you try and arrest him. He can work on desires, you know? It's not mind control, but he can make you want things. Or not want things. And he can manipulate memory. So, play nice?"

"I guess it's fine as long as he doesn't have anyone enslaved in there, and he isn't directly involved in the kidnapping." Jack said. She frowned deeper when Emmaline didn't respond. "He won't have anyone enslaved in there, will he? Like, using his powers to work people's desires and making them love him or be his sex toys?"

"No! He doesn't kidnap people," Emmaline said. There was a pregnant pause before she continued. "Look, he is unseelie trained, so there's a chance there's something weird, but he won't have slaves. Especially not sex slaves, I'm pretty sure he's ace."

"What do you mean, ace?" Jack asked.

"Asexual. Like, he doesn't feel sexual attraction, so the likelihood of him having a sex slave is low," Emmaline said. "I don't know for sure, though."

"Thanks for clarifying," Jack said with deadpan sarcasm, her voice pitched low. Piper smiled through their own trepidation. Of everything they'd learned, most of it had been groundbreakingly weird, but apparently Jack was learning about mundane things, like other identities. It was somewhat comforting.

"Look, it'll be fine. He knows we're coming over. I told him you're both non-magical. So he'll be on his best behaviour, and if you're on your best behaviour, too, this will go fine."

Jack sighed and nodded. They got out of the car and headed up to the green-painted front door. From the car, the door had looked normal, but as they approached Piper saw there were symbols painted on it.

They were painted a colour similar to the green of the door, but with an iridescence. You could only see them when the light hit them at the right angle. It was beautiful.

The symbols seemed to bother Emmaline. She hesitated before knocking on the door, took a breath, and frowned. She repositioned her fist and knocked on a blank spot.

"Deacon, it's me!" she called out.

After a moment, the door opened, and a beautiful man with gorgeous, long, flowing black hair opened the door. His hair almost seemed purple; it was so black. He opened the door a crack and looked out at them, eyes slightly wild, shifting from one foot then to the next with surprising speed.

"Three of you?" He asked.

"Yes, like I said on the phone," Emmaline said.

"I don't trust phones," Deacon said. He stepped back. "Come in, one at a time. You last, Em." His eyes locked with Piper's.

Piper stepped forward, moving through the door without any decision on their part. Why did they move, when they should have waited for Jack to go first? Or Emmaline, who freaking knew magic?

"Deacon, don't. Leave it off," Emmaline said. Piper moved into the house. It smelt of growing plants and something cloying. Heavy perfume?

Jack came through next and looked around, her eyebrows drawn together and her eyes flashing. "What just happened?"

"I didn't," Deacon said, chuckling. "Well, hardly at all."

Emmaline came through last, and Deacon shut the door. Emmaline shuddered and wrapped her arms around herself.

"Are you all right?" Jack asked.

"It's the wards on the door, it's nothing," Emmaline said.

"Our magic can taste quite different, person to person," Deacon said. "Mine is definitely not the flavour of magic Emmaline uses."

"And mine isn't the kind you use," she said, briskly.

"What happened with the door?" Jack asked. "What did you do to Piper?"

"I only used a little compulsion," Deacon said. "Nothing to worry about." He started walking away, deeper into the house.

"Not cool!" Piper said. "Never without my consent!"

"That goes for me, too," Jack said. "Emmaline, is there any way to stop him doing that shit?"

Emmaline kicked Deacon's leg from behind. "Don't be an asshole."

"Okay, okay. Sorry, all." Deacon said. His expression didn't fill Piper with confidence that he wouldn't do it again, though. They'd have to keep an eye on him.

Deacon led them through to a room the next floor up. It was a sitting room with mismatched furniture which had probably been fancy at one point but was now worn.

"What did you want to know, Em? I don't know why you couldn't ask me over the phone." He sat down languidly in a battered-looking velvet armchair and raised his eyebrows.

"Didn't you say you don't trust phones?" Jack asked. Deacon ignored her.

"We're looking for someone called Melchizedek, have you heard of them?" Emmaline asked.

Deacon frowned and tipped his head to one side. "The name is familiar, but I'm afraid I can't quite place it."

"Is this the kind of 'familiar' which would become clear if someone were to cross your palm with silver?" Jack said, her voice dry.

Deacon's face split into a delighted smile. "Where did you find this one, Emmaline? Her will is so strong, it's formidable, but not unbreakable. Not for someone like me."

He smirked at Jack who wavered for a moment and took a step towards the sofa, her eyes locked on Deacon's, glaring.

"Whatever you're doing, you can stop it now," Jack said through gritted teeth.

"Stop it, Deacon!" Emmaline said, shoving him. Jack stepped away from the sofa and moved in between Piper and Deacon.

"We didn't come here for you to use your powers on us," Jack said. "Don't do it again, or we'll have trouble."

Jamie Sands

"What do you want, Deac? Name your price so we can get this over with." Emmaline glared at him.

"For information on finding an information broker?" Deacon grinned and folded his arms in a mockery of Emmaline's posture. "A selfie."

"You want a selfie?" Emmaline shook his head. "No, I don't know what you want with a selfie, but I don't trust that. Ask for something else."

"Fine. I want life force, then. Just a smidge." He gave her a sickly smile, snake oil and wheedling.

"Done," she said. "Give me a vessel."

Deacon nodded and got up to cross the room. Piper's brain struggled to catch up with what Emmaline had just agreed to.

"Wait," Jack said. "Life force? That sounds important, don't give up your life force."

"I'm not giving up mine," Emmaline said, lightly, perhaps slightly amused.

Piper and Jack exchanged uncertain looks. Piper opened their mouth to ask but thought maybe they didn't want the answer. Or at least, not right then.

She followed Deacon to a worktable. It was laden with glass vials, small pots of herbs, and stacks of papers and books with scribbled notes all over them.

Jack and Piper exchanged a look and moved closer to watch. Piper bit their lower lip, they had seen some magic already, but this seemed so much more arcane. So much more like a scene in a horror movie where everything starts to go wrong.

Emmaline pulled out a black glass shape, a twisted pendant which she held mid-air. "This is the life of a white doe," she said. She let the pendant spin some. It caught the light and sparkled like a tiny galaxy.

Deacon peered at it for a moment and then shook his head.

"I'd rather something human."

"Well, I do have this, it's very valuable," Emmaline pocketed the black glass thing and pulled out a string of prayer beads, draping it over her hand. "Several monks gave a little each, enough to fill a bead. How do you like that?"

Deacon smiled and reached to stroke the beads with one finger. Piper leaned closer, too, sure they could see colours playing over the surfaces of the beads. It was enchanting to look at.

"That is lovely," he said.

"The Order of Etienne," Emmaline said. "A hidden monastery in the south of France." She closed her hand over the beads. "But you'd better be able to give us something really good. This is precious to me."

"Of course," he said. He straightened up and clasped his hands together behind his back, like a school boy reciting a poem. "Melchizedek can be found at dusk, under the twisted willow trees down by the water's edge, Blockhouse Bay. The largest tree – it reaches its branches out over the rocks and the water. You can't miss it, or him."

Emmaline handed him the beads. "Thank you, Deacon. See how easy it is when you co-operate and aren't an asshole?"

"You're welcome," he said. He held the beads up to the light and examined them. "Melchizedek will only appear for five minutes, no matter how many are waiting to ask for boons. Rumour has it the hunters have his name now, he doesn't dare stay on this side for longer than that."

"Hunters? Is he a mage or a fairy?" Emmaline asked.

"Yes," Deacon replied. Emmaline frowned.

"Have you heard of anyone called Edith?" Jack asked.

Emmaline and Deacon looked over, startled, as if they'd forgotten they weren't alone in the room.

Deacon's eyes narrowed, thinking. "Doesn't ring a bell."

"Pity," Jack said. "All right, if we're done here?" She looked at Emmaline, who nodded.

"We need to go and speak to some people at the station."

20

The moment they were back in the car, Piper's chest constricted. Their heart raced so fast they thought maybe they were having a heart attack. They leaned their head forward to rest on the steering wheel. They stared at their knees, a roaring in their ears.

"Piper? What's going on?" Emmaline asked.

Piper couldn't answer, they didn't know what was going on. Their mind raced.

Then they realised: it was Deacon. He'd put something in their mind, and he was going to use it to control them. They were in danger, they had to get out of there, but they were meant to be driving and they weren't. They were panicking.

Jamie Sands

Something touched Piper and they flinched, their heart pounding. Piper gripped the steering wheel so hard their knuckles pressed against their skin.

"Shh, it's okay, Piper," Jack said. It was her hand on Piper's back. Piper wasn't at all sure if they wanted it there or not. But Jack's hand started to make slow circles, and that was pretty nice.

Jack and Emmaline said some things to each other but Piper couldn't follow their words. Some car doors opened and shut. Jack leaned in close to Piper, her hand still on their back.

"You're okay now, Piper. Deacon did some shit, but we're safe from him. Emmaline's not that kind of mage. No one's in your mind. Just breathe, okay? Breathe like I am, in and out, slowly." She took a deep slow breath and let it out through her mouth so Piper could hear it.

Piper tried, but their heart was racing so fast. Their breathing was shallow. They closed their eyes and sucked in a deep breath and let it out in a small puff. They tried again with another big breath.

"Let it out, too, Piper," Jack said. "Breathe out as long as you can." Jack's hand as it rubbed circles on Piper's back was a good focus. Piper concentrated on that and exhaled slower this time, working on pushing their air from their lungs.

"That's it, that's really good," Emmaline said. She put a hand on Piper's elbow and Piper opened their eyes to look at her. Emmaline had stopped Deacon doing stuff, right? They could trust her even though she was magic? They could trust her.

But what was that stuff with life essences? That didn't seem on the up and up.

Jamie Sands

Piper turned back to Jack and breathed in time with her again, letting the air *whoosh* out of them and then slowly in through the nose.

"You're doing so well," Jack said. That felt good. Jack's praise meant a lot to Piper. Although – shit, what if freaking out like this meant they were failing their probation? How did you fail probation?

Damnit, their breathing was all fast and panicked again. Piper shook their head and listened to Jack.

"Nothing to worry about," Jack said. Her voice was soft and gentle. Jack was being soft and gentle. What the fuck?

Piper laughed.

"That's it, nothing to worry about," Jack said again.

Piper drew in a deep breath and let it out, shaky. They sat up and opened their eyes. Their heart was still thumping, but it wasn't as bad as it had been. Their mind cleared up some.

Jack pulled her hand back and put it on Piper's shoulder. "How're you doing?"

Piper nodded and looked over at Emmaline, whose face was a picture of concern. "Thanks, I'm okay. Better. Sorry."

"You don't have to apologise," Emmaline said. She squeezed Piper's bicep. "I'd really like to give you a hug."

Piper got out of the car, legs not quite as stable as they'd have liked, and hugged Emmaline. Something about the tiny blonde woman was comforting. Even if she was magic, too, and magic was scary as fuck.

Jack got out of the car and came around to the side, patting Piper on the back as she held on to Emmaline.

After a moment, they let go and swallowed, looking at Jack. They'd messed everything up, losing it at work like that.

"Sorry, Jack," they said. They looked at the ground, and quickly up into Jack's face. Jack shook her head.

"Don't be sorry," she said. "Nothing to be sorry for. Hop in the car, I'll drive us back to the station. You need anything? A juice or something to eat? You can't have a nap because we've got an important interview."

"Heartless!" Emmaline said. "Can't they go back home and you do the interview?"

"No, it's fine," Piper said. "I'll be okay now. I'd rather get on with the day."

Jack gave Emmaline a satisfied look. "See, I know what's best."

"Oh my goddess," Emmaline said. She shoved Jack's arm, playfully. "Are you seriously using this to make yourself look smart?"

Piper laughed, and the laughing made them feel more normal. Emmaline was giggling a little.

"I'm not using it to make myself look smart," Jack said. She lifted her nose into the air and sniffed, but she was smiling, making fun of herself. "I *am* smart. Now, everyone get back in the car and let's get out of here."

21

Emmaline opted to stay out of the police station, and Jack didn't press her for a reason.

She'd wanted to ask Emmaline about what kind of magic she did, but bringing up magic again didn't seem like the best idea so soon after Piper's panic attack.

Daniel's parents had been less than helpful when it came to leads. Or any information at all. Piper and Jack sat outside the interview room. Jack stewed, toying with the silver charms on the bracelet around her wrist as she tried to puzzle them out.

Camille and Richard were distraught about Camille's mother going missing, that much was clear, and they cared deeply for Daniel. *They didn't know where Edith had gone, Jack thought. And yet...*

"They're hiding something," Jack said.

"Do you think so?" Piper looked through the one-way mirror at the two middle-aged people frowning. Camille drank from one of the station's grey tempered glass teacups.

"Yes, But I don't know what it is. They don't know where she is, they're clearly upset. But there's something they're not telling us, and I don't know." She regarded Piper critically. She gauged Piper had recovered from the panic attack earlier, but they were bound to still be shaky. Tired out. But it felt like these two needed a softer touch than Jack could give. "How about you go in there on your own, do the good cop thing, see if you can eke out what it is."

"You want me to go in there?" Piper cleared their throat, looking at Jack with wide eyes.

"Why not? Surely you've talked to suspects before, for other cases?"

Jamie Sands

"Suspects?"

"They're connected to our victim. For all we know, they summoned the dark fey to give them gold or something and the price was dear old granny. Gerard said the dark fey don't kidnap people for no reason."

"Did he say that? I thought he said it was just kind of what they do?"

"I think there's more going on here than a random kidnapping." Jack amended. She glared through the glass at the married couple, as if she could find the answer just by staring.

"You think there's a conspiracy?"

"Get in there, see if you can get them to open up about whatever it is they're talking around."

Piper stood up. "All right, but I don't think this is going to work."

"Ask about Abel, the one who was in prison," Jack said. That might stir them up, get them off-footed enough to let something slip. Jack turned her seat to face the glass.

Piper went into the room and sat with their back to the mirror. "We won't need to keep you much longer."

"We just want to help," Camille said.

"There was one thing Daniel mentioned that we would be interested in following up on," Piper said.

"What was that, dear?" Richard asked. Jack screwed her nose up. Freaking patronising older men.

"He mentioned something about his uncle, your brother, I believe, Camille? I think his name was Abel?"

The expressions on both of Daniel's parent's faces changed from bored but willing to closed off and defensive.

"Bingo," Jack breathed. She licked her lips. How Piper handled this next would make or break the conversation. If Camille and Richard froze up completely, Piper wouldn't get anything out of them no matter what they tried.

"Yes," Camille said, in a clipped manner. "Abel is my brother."

"Daniel said he's working at a library now?"

"That's right, out East somewhere, like Māngere. I'm sure that's not why you brought him up."

"He's previously been in prison?" Piper asked, their voice idle.

"That's right. I'm sure you have the details of what he did." Camille's voice was cold. Richard reached to take her hand.

"Have you seen him recently?"

"No," Camille said. "I haven't spoken to him since the arrest."

"Do you know if he was still in touch with Edith, at all?" Piper asked.

"I have no idea. I'd be surprised if she was in touch with him. She never said anything to me about seeing him, but that doesn't mean she didn't, she could have been hiding it from me." Camille frowned, talking about Abel was clearly distasteful to her.

"Did she hide things from you a lot? I only ask because my own family is awful for keeping secrets. My father was married before he married my mother, and I only recently found out that I have cousins on that side that for some reason we never see," Piper said.

Camille smiled. *Genius*, thought Jack. Making it about her own family really blunted the question.

Jamie Sands

"She had some things she was private about. Things in her past. Edith and Abel were close before. Before, well, all that trouble."

Piper nodded. "And Abel's working at the library. You don't know if there's anything else he's doing? Any groups he's joined?"

"I'm sorry, I have no idea, anything you want to know you'd have to ask him. I haven't seen him in years." Camille folded her hands in her lap and blinked at Piper, clearly trying to signal that this topic was done.

The door behind Jack slammed open and she jumped to her feet, heart racing, hand reaching for the taser on her hip. Coleson walked in.

"Sorry, you're out of time, we need this interview room."

"I beg your pardon? This is an important interview for my missing persons investigation!" Jack folded her arms and glared at Coleson. "Use one of the others."

"Can't, we brought in a suspected killer," Coleson said. "He's in a holding cell now, but we need to get him to talk immediately. Sergeant's approved it."

Jack huffed with frustration. "You're the worst, and you owe me."

Coleson smirked, looking so satisfied that she wanted to punch him then and there. Instead, she turned, opened the door to the interview room, and smiled tightly at the Armstrongs.

"Thanks so much for your time today. Looks like we need to give up the room now."

Jamie Sands

Piper made a tiny, frustrated noise. Camille stood up immediately and picked up her purse. Richard took Camille's elbow, and they left quickly.

"Could we just talk in the office?" Piper asked. Jack shook her head.

"The Armstrongs are ready to leave now, I think," Jack said. "Thanks for your time today."

22

Piper got home and had a long, hot shower.

"What a day," they said to the little duck that sat on the sill in the bathroom. Their bathroom was nice enough, if a little old, and the shower was installed over the bath itself. *Probably,* Piper thought, *I should have had a bath. Baths are good for unwinding the nerves, and I had a lot of nerves today.*

But if they'd had a bath, they would have lingered in it, refilling the hot water and soaking for hours. Possibly with a podcast or an audiobook on. Which wouldn't be a problem, except they hadn't eaten dinner yet.

Food was important for staying calm, Piper had learnt this the hard way. Food and water. Without them, things got a lot harder and Piper's head started to hurt and they got faint and obviously, really hangry. No, food and drink were important, but Piper had needed to wash the sweat and grime of the day off their skin.

They rinsed off under the super-hot shower water and then shut it off, towelling themself dry and eying themself in the mirror. The mirror was fogged up from the shower's steam, but they could still make out the shape of their reflection. It didn't feel like a solid surface all of a sudden. It felt like a dangerous window, one which could fly open at any time and let out... what? Ghosts? Goblins? Strange men who sounded English and got up to god knows what at parties?

Piper hurried out of the bathroom and into the bedroom, wrapped in their towel, hoping they weren't dripping too much on the carpet. There was a mirror in the bedroom, too, of course, but that one was easily covered with a scarf. Piper changed into their flannel pyjama pants and an oversized hoodie.

Dinner was oven fries and frozen chicken tenders and took about twenty minutes. While the food cooked, Piper put away the dishes from the dishrack, tidied up the cutlery drawer, and made themselves an extra-large cup of chamomile tea.

Chamomile for the nerves, because even though their heart wasn't racing, they didn't quite feel at home or comfortable yet.

They pulled out their phone and tapped a quick message to their brother.

Yo, bro, you still awake?

Ben replied within seconds.

It's 7pm. So, yes I'm awake

Piper smiled and felt a little of the tension lift from their shoulders.

I dunno, you get up at like four in the morning, I don't know when your bedtime is.

He sent back a laughing emoji and another message.

What's up, Pipes? You lonely? You want to call?

They breathed out and nodded.

Yep, will call you as soon as I have my dinner sorted.

Once they had dinner on a plate and some sauce on the side, Piper carried it to the couch, propped their phone on the stand on the table, and called their brother.

Ben picked up after a few seconds. At the sight of his shaggy brown hair, his long straight nose, and his warm hazel eyes, Piper instantly felt a little better.

"Hey, you," he said.

"Hey bro," she said. "How's my favourite brother?"

"I'm your only brother," he said, laughing. It was so good to see his smile, to hear his laughter, that Piper almost teared up. They stuffed a fry in their mouth to smother the emotion.

"I'm good," he said, and grinned at the camera. "My bakery had a write-up in the local paper!"

"Impressive," Piper said through a mouth of potato.

"It was a really nice write-up. Mum's cut it out and filed it away somewhere." Ben laughed again and shook his head. "Ridiculous."

"You deserve it, though. I miss your chocolate eclairs. I haven't been able to find anything nearly as good up here yet."

"I'd offer to send you some but I don't think the cream would travel." He sat back and smiled at her. "How's the new job?"

Jamie Sands

Piper bit their lip, they couldn't exactly go into any of the details with him. Best just to keep it high level.

"Um, challenging. It's challenging, but in a good way. Jack Duarte is just exactly how I imagined her and I love her. Not like a romantic way, though, just like, in a mentor kind of way."

"Okay, good. And the others are... okay?" He was skirting the issue, not wanting to ask outright if the new station was full of bullies, but both of them knew that's what he was referring to.

"Well, there are some who aren't exactly nice, but nothing like the old station." Piper speared a piece of chicken and ate it, hoping he wouldn't want to ask more about that. Honestly, it just felt good to see his face. He grounded them. "Tell me, how's your love life?"

Ben shook his head and frowned. "A desolate wasteland, exactly the same as when you left, thanks so much for reminding me."

"It's good to see you, baby bro."

"Good to see you, too, call me again, okay? Soon. I miss your face."

"I miss yours, too." Suddenly, Piper felt like crying over the remains of their chicken tenders. Ben sounded like he wanted to say goodbye and they weren't sure they'd gotten everything they needed out of the conversation. "Hey Ben, I sorta... no details, because you know, crime and stuff, but I had something sort of blow my mind today."

"Expand your worldview, maybe?" he suggested.

Piper nodded. "Big time."

"I knew it'd happen, Auckland's a really different place to Christchurch, after all."

Piper felt a sudden ache of longing for the town they knew so well. The river and the park and the biting cold in the early morning. But this was their life now, and they had to do what they could to make it work.

"Any advice?" they asked.

"Get a dog?" Ben suggested. He grinned, shook his head, and continued. "For real, though, it's just like any time something freaks you out. Look after your basic needs first. Food, water, rest."

"Well, I'm on the way," Piper said. They waved a chicken tender at Ben and took a bite out of it.

"Great, good. After a bit of time, things will seem easier. Just as long as you're safe, obviously. Then it's deep breathing exercises, meditation, go for a run, you know. Or like, call me. You'll adjust, this too shall pass, all of that."

"How did you get so wise?" Piper asked, sighing and slumping back on the couch.

"It's all the time I spend with dough, before the bakery opens," he said. "Really gives you time to think."

They shared another laugh. "Take care, bro."

"You take care, and call me again soon, okay?"

For a moment, once Ben had hung up the call, Piper felt overwhelmingly lonely and cold, but the feeling passed, and they tidied up their dinner dishes and put on some music to keep them company.

New city, new apartment, new partner, new station, new case... and on top of all that? New information about the very fabric of the universe?

Jamie Sands

Too much going on at once, Piper thought. Just put the dishes on the rack and then go flop on the couch with the TV. Or go straight to bed with a book. Ben's right, rest and a bit of time to process are what I need.

23

Piper got to the station on their own the next day, and although they anticipated they'd sleep late, they found themself waking early, as if a habit had already formed. Still, it had been nice to take some time with their morning routine and make their own way down to the station. Seeing Ben's face, and his sensible advice, had done wonders for their mood.

"Morning, Piper."

"Good morning, Jack!"

Jack was already at her desk and handed Piper a stack of files to sort through. For about half an hour, they worked in silence.

Jamie Sands

"I think we really need to talk to Abel," Piper said, chewing on their lip. They sat at Jack's desk. Jack was typing some notes into the case files about the interview.

"And Melchizedek at dusk," Jack checked her watch. "I don't know if we have time to do both, but we can look up Abel's file and check through it. The initial case records said he had a solid alibi for the time of Edith's disappearance, though, that's why I didn't request he come in."

"What was the alibi?"

"He was reading a book to a class of twenty-five kids at the library. Year threes, which is, uh, seven- and eight-year-olds."

"That's a lot of witnesses." Piper brought up the file on their laptop, scanning through it. "And he was imprisoned for murder, initially. Did you know that?"

Jack leaned on the back of Piper's chair, her arm brushing Piper's arm as she read over their shoulder.

"Reverend Zebedee said it was murder, but I don't think he'd be in a public service position unless it was manslaughter or he was acquitted or something. Have you got the details there?" Her voice trailed off as they both read the same bit of information.

"That'll be why Camille doesn't speak to him anymore."

"His sister's lover." Piper breathed out. "How horrible. I wonder why?"

"And on the appeal he was acquitted for... coercion? We need to talk to Abel." Jack tapped the back of the chair and straightened up. "Bring up the witness statements and see what else you can find out. I'll call him about an interview later tonight or tomorrow."

Piper got to work, scan-reading file after file, plugging in a pair of headphones and listening to some of the testimony at the court. When Jack returned, she brought coffee, and sat down next to them, handing them a cup.

Piper rubbed their eyes and pulled the headphones off. "Thanks for the coffee."

"What'd you find?"

"There's something strange about it. There seemed to be a motive, because Edith didn't approve of Eddy, but the reason doesn't sound convincing. She says she didn't like the look of him when she was questioned about it. Camille's testimony is short. She cries about Eddy, says her mother didn't approve, and she can't understand why Abel would do it. Then, when Abel's questioned about why he did it, he says he got angry. They ask him over and over – apparently they'd got on well before, but he's stubborn. Keeps on saying he got angry and he lost control."

"Sounds weird. So whatever it is that Camille and Richard wouldn't talk about, they didn't talk about back then, either."

"Seems not."

"The appeal hearing was different, he said he was under influence from the church they were in, that they brainwashed him and he wasn't acting in his right mind. They acquitted him."

"Good work, Piper. Impressive." Jack patted them on the shoulder. "We got about a half hour before we need to pick up Emmaline and head out to Blockhouse Bay, so how about grabbing a bite?"

"You don't grab a bite, you get a bite," Piper said, standing up.

"And what do you do with a pedant?" Jack said, and Piper could have sworn she was teasing them.

Jamie Sands

"You buy them pizza at Viv's."

"Sounds like a deal."

24

Emmaline met them at Viv's pizza parlour where Piper was happily tucking into a gigantic slice of pepperoni. Jack ate more slowly, enjoying a slice of bacon and mushroom. Emmaline sat down, peered at the selection of slices they had in front of them, and pulled a face.

"Did you only get meat pizzas?"

Jack raised her eyebrows. "Yes?"

Em got up and went to order, returning shortly with a slice of margherita and another one which seemed to be only cheese.

"Is that one only cheese?" Jack asked.

"You say it like it's a bad thing," Emmaline took a long sniff of the hot pizza. "*Quattro formaggi* is a gift from the Italian gods. It's all cheese and cheese is delicious." She bit into it.

"That's a good point," Piper said. "Cheese is delicious."

"This afternoon we learnt that Edith's son killed his sister's lover, but we don't know why. How did your day go?" Jack said.

"My brother got back in touch, finally," Emmaline said. "He's willing to bring us through to Faerie. Tonight, if you like."

Jack and Emmaline blinked at her.

"Us? Through to there?" Piper swallowed. "Is that what we want to do?"

"I'm not sure," Jack said. "There does seem to be a connection to... there, in this case, that's for sure. What would we do over there?"

"Chances are that Melchizedek will give us a name or something to look up, and that will be in Faerie, not over this side. Raphael will do the enchantment to take us over, after we've met with Melchey." Emmaline flipped her hair over her shoulder.

"Melchey?" Piper asked. "I thought you didn't know him."

"I don't. I didn't, but I get sick of saying his whole name, it's so complicated."

"I don't know if I want to go into another universe," Jack mumbled, picking at her pizza before taking a bite.

"I guess... I mean, it's scary, but it's an adventure," Piper said, smiling some. "I'm afraid about it, but I want to do it. I mean, you can't get more spooky than going to another dimension and to meet fairies."

Jack sighed and rubbed her forehead. "Are you sure you're gonna be all right with this?" She looked at Piper. "After Deacon, you kind of had a meltdown." She didn't say it unkindly, and Piper remembered the way Jack had looked after them while they were panicking. She'd said all the right things.

"I don't know. But I don't think it'll be like with Deacon. None of them will be in my head, right?" Piper asked, looking at Emmaline.

"No, it'll be different. The fey will try and get you to agree to things, not just jump in."

"So, mages are ruder than the fey?"

"Mages aren't rude," Emmaline said. She chewed her lip. "Okay, I guess some are. In general, the fey have some rules, mages are meant to as well, but there's dark and light to everyone. You know what? Raphael can explain this better."

Piper finished off their pizza and sat back, rubbing their face. They'd sounded brave earlier talking about adventure, but Jack had made a good point about their ability to cope. "I don't want to freak out and let you two down."

"To be honest, I think freaking out in this situation makes sense. But that said, if you panic in the middle of something, that'd be a problem," Jack said. She sighed and shrugged one shoulder. "But if you think you can handle it, I'd like to have you along."

"Do you want to go home and let us handle the rest of this stuff?" Emmaline asked. She patted Piper's arm and somehow it was comforting and not condescending.

Piper looked between the two of them and shook their head. "No. I want to help. I can help. I'll never know if I don't try, right?"

"That's the spirit, partner," Jack said.

25

The three of them drove to Blockhouse Bay Beach Reserve a half hour before the sun went down. Jack was on edge, cautious and watchful. She'd forgotten that the worst thing about having a partner was having someone else to worry about.

It was bad enough doing shit on her own, but with Piper along for the ride, she had to ensure they were protected and safe. Then, there was Emmaline, who Jack was starting to get a soft spot for.

A soft spot was a bad idea, all around, but regardless. Now she had to protect Emmaline as well.

Feelings for Emmaline were troubling. Jack had learnt from Marlo that she wasn't equipped to deal with long-term relationships. Growing up, Jack had always lived with her father, seeing her mother maybe once a year, and she'd never seen her dad in any relationship. She was aware she had no idea how a good relationship should look.

And the fact Marlo still thought it was okay to drop around and share Jack's dinner...

Love wasn't a thing that Jack could do. It didn't work, she wasn't going to go there with Emmaline. It wasn't a thing.

But the way that Emmaline laughed was absolutely charming. Her eyes were bright, and they actually sparkled. She was kind and no nonsense, and those two things were important to Jack after what she'd been through with Marlo.

They got out of the car and walked under the trees by the water's edge as the sun went down.

"I think it's this one," Emmaline said. She turned from examining a large tree and gave Jack a wide smile. Jack's heart thumped, and she felt warmth spread through her chest. She blinked and turned away, trying to suck in some deep breaths and get a hold of herself.

She had hired Emmaline for a case, that's all that their relationship was. It'd be wrong to make it more when it was supposed to be professional.

Piper shifted nervously from foot to foot beside Jack, humming softly.

"Is there anything we should know before we meet this guy?" Jack asked.

"Let me think. If he's fey, you shouldn't accept any food from him, and don't agree to anything. Like, if he offers you something, don't take it." Emmaline said.

"How will we know if he's fey?" Piper said.

"I'll know. And if he asks you to promise him anything, you say no. Got that?" Emmaline peered into both their faces.

"No promises, no food, no agreeing," Piper said. "Sounds easy enough."

"It's not as easy as all that."

Jack turned towards the unfamiliar voice to see the hunched figure of a man. He looked rough. He wore many layers of tatty, dirty clothes, and his hands were covered with fingerless gloves. "If you want to stay safe from the good folk, you must know their ways."

Piper made a soft squeaking noise and Emmaline moved forward, putting herself between him and Piper. "He's fey."

"I think I could tell myself," Jack said.

"Melchizedek, I presume?" Emmaline said to the stranger.

"That's right," he replied. He smiled and either his teeth had been filed to points, or they had always been pointy. "What can I help three lovely young ladies with tonight?"

"Not a lady," Piper mumbled.

"We need information on the disappearance of a woman, called Edith Armstrong," Jack said. "Has she been taken to Faerie?"

"Maybe I know about that, maybe I don't," Melchizedek said. His lips parted in a rictus grin which pulled his cheeks up unpleasantly and he took a step towards Jack.

"What's your price? We want to know if you saw her go through, and who she was with," Jack said. She didn't much care for the way Melchizedek seemed to think he could scare them.

"And where she is now," Piper added, their voice thin.

"My price?" He seemed to consider for a moment. "Something that sparkles. Something precious."

Piper, Emmaline, and Jack all exchanged looks. Piper's hand went to the thin gold chain around their throat. A charm hung from it.

Jack hated the thought of Piper giving up something important on their first case. Impulsively, she shook her head at Piper and held up her wrist, pulling her shirt sleeve up to display the silver charm bracelet with a couple of dangling charms. Her heart thudded at the thought of giving it up, but it was better than the alternatives.

"Would this do?"

Melchizedek leaned in to examine it closely.

Jack could smell the damp soil scent of him. His proximity made the hairs on her arms stand on end. The ancient, reptile part of her brain started to tell her to run. That this thing wasn't natural; it was a predator. She ignored the urge to flee and squared her shoulders.

He straightened up. "Yes, I like that."

Jack worked to remove it. The clasp fought her, stiff because she left it on most of the time. Now that she was taking it off, she felt a thrill of freedom. It was exhilarating, and she smiled when she looked up at the fey again.

"Give us the information first, then you can have it."

Melchizedek sniffed once. "Fine. There's a gang of dark fey, pixies, sidhe, and sluagh who kidnap mortals for money. They say there's a great deal of profit to be made. They work for those fey and mortals who can afford it, moving here and there."

"Mortals pay?" Jack asked. "For what?"

"Aye. To be kidnapped, to be taken to our realm, to participate in our revels and taste our mead." The fey nodded, as if this was obvious. "Many yearn for something more than they can have on this side of the mirror."

"They ask to be kidnapped by dark fey?" Piper asked, aghast.

"Not solely dark fey. Fey of all courts enjoy a tasty mortal." Melchizedek said. "And they have other services."

"Could someone pay them to kill?" Jack asked.

"All they used to do was kill," Melchizedek said, somewhat wistfully. "I'm sure you've heard the old stories."

Jack wondered how many of the mysterious murder cases in her past were unexplainable because of fairy assassins.

"Okay, this gang, do you have any names or a way to track them down?"

"You can summon an envoy by speaking to the reflection of the moonlight. Say the words key, lock, freedom, entrapment; and then ask very politely for someone to visit you. Not necessarily in that order." He winked at Piper, who shied further behind Emmaline.

Emmaline pulled a face. "That sounds like summoning them for their services. I don't want to start a bargain without talking to them. What about if we can get to Faerie, is there a name we can ask around for?"

Melchizedek looked annoyed. Jack wondered if Emmaline had caught him out.

"*Lachrimosa.* If you say the word *Lachrimosa* you'll get their attention." He held his hand out for the bracelet which Jack placed in his palm, careful not to touch his skin with her skin.

"Thank you, that was helpful." Jack gave him a polite smile. "I hope we can do business again sometime."

"It would be my pleasure," he said. His eyes were on the bracelet which he dangled in his fingers, examining it closely. "Run along now, in case another wants to deal with sweet Melchizedek this evening."

Jack raised her eyebrows and turned to leave.

"What was the bracelet?" Emmaline asked once they were in the car. She'd climbed into the passenger seat and Piper was in the back. Jack wondered if they'd discussed it, somehow.

"It was nothing," Jack said, hoping it was enough to deflect the question. *It wasn't.*

"But you wore it all the time," Piper said. "Where'd it come from?"

Jack was silent for a moment, putting the car into gear and driving away. She ran a hand through her hair. How was this question more nerve-wracking than dealing with an actual being from another dimension?

"It was a gift from my ex, a couple of Christmases ago. She'd give me a charm for my birthday. Then we broke up, and I stopped getting charms, but I was used to wearing it, I guess. I dunno, I probably should've got rid of it ages ago."

Jamie Sands

Emmaline frowned some. "You shouldn't have given away something with sentimental value. I had things to bargain with."

"You'd already given up something precious for this case, it was my turn." Jack gave her what she hoped was a reassuring smile.

"Precious?" Emmaline tilted her head. "You mean the beads from the monastery? I have a few of those, and a contact inside. I can get more of them whenever."

Jack shrugged a shoulder. "Still, it's fine. She's my ex for a reason. No need to hold on to mementoes."

"We could go to a cheap jewellery place and buy up a bunch of really sparkly things to trade with?" Piper said. "Would that help?"

"We can ask Raphael about it. That reminds me." Emmaline

pulled out her phone and checked it. "He's at his local place,

head downtown."

Jack turned the car and looked over at Emmaline. "This is

your brother who's half fey? He lives here?"

"Fey trained," Emmaline said. "All human. Mage. And no, he

doesn't live here. But he can travel through Faerie easily. He

rented a small apartment here when I moved, so he could

visit with me. Come on, let's go see him."

26

They pulled up to a tall, newish apartment building. To Jack it looked the same as a half-dozen other buildings in this part of town. Emmaline glanced at Google Maps on her phone and glanced up at the building.

"This is it, and he says fourth floor. I'll know which door when I see it." They got out of the car.

Piper sighed, pulling their hair back into a ponytail. "All we've done for days is talk to people and get a clue to go and talk to someone else."

Jack slapped them on the back and chuckled. "That's how this job works, rookie. Unfortunately, it's not how it is on TV with DNA samples and a eureka moment. Sorry."

"No, I know. I guess I'm tired." Piper sighed, then stifled a yawn.

"I don't know exactly what's about to happen," Jack said. "But it's probably going to be dangerous. If you want to head home and sleep, go for it. I'll catch you up in the morning."

"Nuh-uh!" Piper said. "You're not going to get rid of me. I transferred over so I could see all the weird shit you see, and I'm not heading home to go to bed."

"Fine, but don't forget I gave you this out," Jack said. She really had no way to predict if they'd be safe with Emmaline's brother, although she trusted Emmaline, she certainly didn't trust the fey they'd just met. And this brother was fey trained...

"I want you both to meet my brother. He's charming," Emmaline said. "And I'm sure he can answer your questions about the fey."

They went to the fourth floor. Emmaline homed in on one door. To Jack's eye it was the same plain grey as the rest of the doors, but she smiled and traced a finger over it before knocking.

After a few moments, the door opened, and a handsome blond man with similar bright blue eyes to Emmaline opened the door. She threw herself at him. He caught her with a laugh and hugged her tight.

"Emmy, how are you? You didn't sell your name to the fey you met, did you?"

"I may have been born at night, but it wasn't *last* night." Emmaline kissed his cheek and he kissed hers, before they both turned back to the other two. "This is Jack and Piper, they're the detectives I've been working with."

"Please, come in." Raphael pulled the door wide open. "If you feel a weird shiver when you come in, it's fine, it's just my wards." He had the same mixed-up accent that his sister had

– partially English, partially French, and with a touch of American in there as well.

"You have so many wards," Emmaline said, her voice full of wonder. "More than normal."

"Life's been interesting." Raphael moved into the apartment and crossed to the kitchen to put the kettle on.

"Is tea a mage thing or a family thing?" Piper asked. They leaned into Jack. "Did you feel anything when you came through the door?"

Jack shook her head. "Not a thing."

"Neither," Piper grumbled.

"Can it be both?" Raphael asked. "If you don't want tea maybe you'd prefer Earl Grey or peppermint? I'm afraid I don't have any milk."

"Earl Grey, I guess," Piper said.

"I'm fine without tea," Jack said. She looked around the room. It was quite sparse, as if he'd rented it furnished and brought in very few of his own things. There was a tall bookcase with a few books on it and some notebooks which looked to be well thumbed. A tall mirror stood leaning against one of the walls.

Over by the window, there was a row of potted herbs. It didn't seem like he spent enough time in this place to keep plants alive, but they looked leafy and green.

Soon everyone had a cup of tea, even Jack, who was given one despite her disinterest. They sat down around a kitchen table half covered with papers, books, and pens.

"Sorry about the mess," Raphael said. "I'm never very organised, and Amy's still resting more than she does anything else."

"Is she here?" Emmaline asked, perking up. Raphael shook his head. Emmaline pouted into her tea.

"She's at Gerard's house in Faerie," he said.

"Who's Amy?" Piper asked.

"My new girlfriend," Raphael said. "So, uh, what exactly is it you're wanting to do?"

"I think we need to go to Faerie," Emmaline said. "There's a chance the woman these two are looking for is over there."

"What if she went voluntarily?" Piper asked, louder than they'd intended. "I mean, Melchizedek said some humans ask to be taken."

"Then why leave the note?" Jack asked.

"And she'd just been in touch with Daniel," Piper added, frowning.

"If she went willingly, I want to hear that from her. I want to find her and speak to her," Jack said.

Raphael frowned, tapping his finger on his chin. "I don't love the idea of you going into Faerie to wander around looking for someone with no leads."

"We don't have *no* leads," Jack said, sipping her tea before setting the cup back down because she really didn't want it. "We have the name of the group who kidnapped her."

"And I can take a spirit or two along with us for protection," Emmaline said. Jack looked at Emmaline. Maybe it was time to ask what kind of magic Emmaline did.

"You know to stick to the path, yes?" He looked at Emmaline, and she nodded.

"Yes, big brother. If you're this worried, why don't you just come with us?"

Raphael chewed his lower lip, considering it. "I'd love to, but Amy's pretty delicate still. I don't like leaving her for too long."

Jack wondered what Amy was delicate from, but it wasn't what they needed to be talking about that moment. "All right, what else do we need to know?"

"You'll need to think about the kinds of things you're willing to part with. You'll want to bargain to get information. The fey will ask for your freedom, your life, and your name. They're not things you want to give, obviously." He frowned, twisting his mouth to the side and thinking for a moment before continuing. "They also might ask for the way it felt when you first saw the sea, or the shine out of your hair. Those are things which aren't going to be too badly missed, and it's less dangerous to agree to them."

Jamie Sands

Jack shifted in her chair, not at all sure that she wanted to hand over memories – if such a thing was even possible? Raphael was talking about it so casually, though, so it had the ring of sincerity. She didn't doubt what he was saying, even if she couldn't quite get her head around it.

"The shine out of my hair?" Piper asked. "How do they even do that?"

"Magic, love," Raphael said. He smiled warmly at Piper. "It's everywhere there. We think it's the source of magic in this world, what we have – Em and me – and other mages, it's what trickles through." He shook his head, catching himself rambling, possibly? "So, stick to the path. If you must deal with dark fey be extra careful about not promising things or agreeing to anything. Maybe... Maybe you should get Gerard to go with you. He'd be a good shield from the really weird shit and he knows how to speak with the dark fey."

"Do you think he'd do it?" Jack asked, quickly. At least they'd spoken to Gerard before. "I mean, the more protection we can get in la-la land the happier I'd be."

"You'd have to ask him, see how busy he is." Raphael sipped his tea and then gave her a half smile. "He'd be willing to help if he has the time."

"Sure, I can ask." Emmaline said. "You're not going to go all protective big brother and try to stop me?"

"Why would I do that?" Raphael shrugged one shoulder. "You're a grown-ass woman now, you can do what you want. Besides, you'd find some other way to get over there if I didn't help. At least I know my way is safe."

He stood up and took down a ball of string and a knife from the shelf near the door, bringing them back to the table. "I'll make you some charms. Wrist, Em, let me do yours first so these two can see it's safe."

"Thanks," Emmaline said, nodding.

Piper leaned their chin on their hand to watch closely. Jack watched Piper to see how they reacted to the practice of magic. But Raphael seemed nice, surely his magic wouldn't freak them out the way Deacon's had.

Raphael cut a length of string off the ball and looped it a couple of times around Emmaline's wrist. As he wound it a third time, he sang a few lines in French. He had a pleasant voice, melodic and clear. All three of them watched as he knotted the string in a complicated way and tapped the knot with one finger.

"There you go. Who's next?"

Piper looked at Jack and cleared their throat, their eyes large.

Jack moved her chair closer to Raphael's. "Me. My partner isn't too comfortable with magic, just yet."

"I'd be interested to know if you feel anything when I do this. Emmaline can feel magic being used, of course, and Amy does too, but she's not really normal." He repeated the whole ritual, wrapping the string around her wrist and singing a song.

He sat back. "Feel anything?"

Jack sucked on her lower lip, taking stock of her body. "I really didn't. I wanted to, and I tried, but..." She paused, thinking it through. "Nah. I feel a string. Your turn, Piper."

Piper switched seats with Jack and offered up their wrist. "Do you do this a lot?" They asked him.

"String magic? I dabble in it. I sell some of my string charms in a magic shop in the States. It's way more effective than it looks like it will be. And when you're back you can unravel the knot to break the spell." Raphael began winding the string around their wrist.

Jamie Sands

"And what exactly is this spell doing?" Piper asked.

"Protection. It's sort of like a message to the fey telling them you're linked to me, and if anything happens to you, I'll know about it," he said.

"And they all know who you are?" Jack asked, a little incredulous.

"Not at all. But the incantation has an imprint of my magic. So they'll be able to sense a human mage, trained by the Raven King, and that I have a bit of power." He tied off the knot and grinned at Piper. "All done."

"My brother, the humble," Emmaline said. "A *bit* of power. Ever since the incident with the Heart of Magic, you've been buzzing with godlike abilities." She rolled her eyes in an affectionate way.

Raphael shrugged and smiled. "Well. It'll help, anyway. Do you need anything before we cross over? Food or rest or...?"

Emmaline looked at Jack and Piper. "I'm all right, how about you two?"

"I think I'm too hyped to eat or rest or anything. Let's go," Jack said. Her heart had sped up, and she could feel adrenaline, like she was close to breaking a case or something.

"Do you remember the rules I told you?" Raphael looked between Jack and Piper.

"Stay on the path," Jack said.

"Don't agree to anything or make promises," Piper added.

"No trading freedom, name, or your life. And don't eat anything unless Gerard offers it to you. They have food from over here. Same with drinks from anyone but him, they're no good." Raphael put his hands on his hips and nodded. "Those are the big ones."

"What happens if you eat or drink something?" Jack asked.

"You'd start turning fey." Emmaline said.

Piper's eyes widened. "Turning fey is a bad thing, right?"

"Bad." Emmaline said.

"If you turn fey you become magic, and if you become magic, you won't be able to live in this world permanently again. You'd be tied to Faerie," Raphael added. "The other thing is you can't know what turning magic would look like for you. For some, it's magical powers; and for others, it's constantly freezing, or turning everything you touch into gold, or every word you say comes out of your mouth as a toad. Utterly unpredictable."

"Definitely bad," Piper said. They pulled a face and shuddered.

"There was something else," Jack said, as a memory came to the front of her mind. "Melchizedek mentioned some kinds of things. One of them was pixies, which I have heard of. But the other things?"

"Sluagh and sidhe," Emmaline said. "He mentioned those names."

"Those are species, not names. Hmm, sluagh," Raphael wrinkled his nose. "They're thought to be spirits of people who were so evil they couldn't get into Heaven, Hell, or Limbo. Earth itself rejected them, so they ended up in Faerie. They like to spread these stories about themselves, anyway, I don't know how true it is. They're nasty." He finished his tea and then continued. "The sidhe are more of a general name for the more traditional kind of fairies or elves. If you imagine the elves in Tolkien, that's close. There are lots of types, but generally they swan around acting like they're better than everyone else."

"Totally horrifying," Piper breathed. Jack patted their back.

"It's alright, we have some pieces of string to protect us, remember?" Jack said.

"That's not as comforting as you think it is," Piper grumbled.

"If sidhe are like Tolkien elves, does that make pixies like Tinkerbell?" Jack asked.

"Yeah, pretty much." Raphael said. "They're fun-loving, they can shapeshift all tiny. They jingle a little sometimes, too, we think J.M. Barrie probably went to Faerie and met one – he might've even been a mage."

"Far out," Piper said.

"It's a lot to take in, isn't it?" Emmaline said. She nudged Piper's arm with her elbow. "You okay?"

"It's ridiculous." Piper rolled their eyes and nudged Emmaline back. "But yeah, I'm okay."

"Is everyone sorted?" Raphael stood and led them to the full-length dress mirror in the corner of the room. "I'll open the portal. Emmy goes through first, then you two, and I'll come last and close it up again. Got it? We'll come through right by Gerard's house. Don't wander off."

He pressed his palm on the mirror and pulled a silver cased cigarette lighter from his pocket with his other hand. He spoke three words in a language Jack had never heard before, and the mirror's surface transformed into a fiery, glowing doorway.

He nodded to Emmaline who winked at Jack before stepping through. Jack followed, tugging Piper through behind her.

27

Piper's heart raced. If there was one thing they wanted to learn from Jack, it was how to be so self-assured. The woman was unflappable. Sure, she got annoyed, but no matter what happened she took it in her stride.

Piper, on the other hand, was shaking. Sure, she'd said she was okay, but they'd just watched a man open a mirror portal to another dimension. Then, they'd walked through the mirror into that other dimension.

They knew they were in another dimension because there was a smell in the air they'd never smelt before, and when they looked up, the stars made no sense. They were certainly not the stars Piper had looked at from Earth.

There were blank patches in the sky, where there were no stars at all. In other parts of the sky the stars were moving in slow arcs and spirals. And they weren't just silvery gold, there were red ones and blue ones and purple ones.

Piper grabbed for Jack's hand and clutched it. Jack didn't seem to notice.

"This is the path." Raphael pointed at the ground.

They stood on a worn, flat path through grass and shrubs. It was clear, and seemed to glow ever so slightly.

"It goes right through Faerie. If you have a clear intention of where you want to go, it'll take you there, eventually. It branches off. When you come to a fork, just trust your gut," Raphael said.

"Maybe you could guide us through?" Emmaline said, turning to her brother and making her eyes all big at him. *Such a younger sibling move,* Piper thought.

"Please? I mean, you know so much about it all and I know almost nothing."

"Yeah, all right. I can take you some of the way, but if you're going to go into any Court land I can't follow, I'm too tied to the Raven King, and he's a free fey. They won't–" He stopped himself from whatever he'd been about to say, then said, "be polite to me."

"If it's that dangerous, don't worry about it," Emmaline said, changing her tone instantly from pleading, helpless little sister to self-assured. "I have a couple tricks up my sleeve if anything happens."

"No, I'll take you a little of the way. That right there is Gerard's house." He pointed at a quaint brick cottage. Piper took a long look at it, memorising it.

"Aw, it's exactly how I imagined," Emmaline said, clasping her hands together.

"I think I had a fairy tale storybook which had this exact house in one of the illustrations," Piper said. "I think it was Grandma's cottage in Red Riding Hood."

Raphael chuckled. "I wouldn't be surprised if Gerard had the same book and designed the house to match it. He's a big reader."

"So, we come back here by following the path?" Jack asked. Her hand was on the pepper spray and baton holster on her belt. Piper felt for their own weapon, they weren't at all sure if either weapon would be any good against the fey, though.

"That's right. The path will lead you back here. Eventually."

"Which way do we go to start?" Emmaline asked. She spun on the spot, looking all around.

"I have a good feeling about this way," Raphael said. He started walking. As they followed, Piper realised they were still holding on to Jack's hand.

Jamie Sands

"Sorry," Piper said, letting go.

"No, it's all right," Jack said, taking Piper's hand again. "I guess we're not in Kansas anymore. You let me know if you want to bail, okay?"

Piper nodded, feeling bolstered. By all rights, they should be panicking again at this, but Jack's presence beside them was soothing. The option to bail and get back to their world was a comfort, as well. They followed Raphael down the path.

"The code word we had was *Lachrimosa*," Emmaline said. She slipped her arm through Raphael's.

"Doesn't ring a bell," he said lightly, as if they were talking about the newest Hollywood movie blockbuster. "But it's not like I know everyone, far from it."

"How've you been?" she asked him.

"I'm okay. Lots of meditation and healing Amy as much as I can, but, y'know, it's going to take a while." He glanced over his shoulder, checking Piper and Jack were still behind him, possibly. Or looking back towards Gerard's house, where Piper assumed Amy was.

"You really like her, huh?" Emmaline asked. She nudged him. He smiled down at her. His manner with her reminded Piper of Ben which was swiftly followed by a pang of missing him. They should really give him a call when they get back.

Assuming they get back. That thought was unpleasant, and Piper dismissed it instantly.

They'd get back. And they'd call their brother and ask him how his plans for moving to Auckland were coming. Because he hadn't spoken about it last time they talked, and they really wanted him nearby.

"Swing by after you do what you gotta do, and you can probably meet her," Raphael said. Piper wondered if they'd spaced out and missed some of the conversation. They'd dropped Jack's hand at some point, too. They rubbed their forehead and took a deep breath. Focus on the here and now.

Piper's eyes wandered from the two siblings to the landscape surrounding the path. It was a sparsely wooded area, with long grass and low bushes. Here and there things moved, rustling the underbrush and making noises. Some of the noises seemed like animal sounds, some like whispered words. A pair of glowing eyes appeared, peering around a tree trunk. Piper looked away quickly, grabbing on to Jack's arm with both their hands.

"I probably shouldn't make eye contact with any of the things I can see, right?" Piper asked, their voice coming out as a whisper.

"I get the feeling we shouldn't do anything which draws attention," Jack said softly, matching Piper's volume.

There were noises up ahead, some kind of gentle uproar. A lot of different voices, singing, and cursing, but not the roar of a riot.

The trees that lined the road began to sprout flags and bunting and slowly they began to see stalls set up under the branches. There was also more foot traffic on and off the path – the bustle of dozens of bodies moving about was unsettling to Piper.

"Shit, the market," Raphael said. He cleared his throat and when he spoke again his voice was brighter. "If we're lucky, the people you need to talk to will be here, nice and easy to find."

"A market? The Goblin Market? Like in that poem?" Jack asked.

"The very one," Raphael said.

"That's pretty perfect for us, right? Lots of fey all in the same place?" Jack said, hopefully.

"Lots of them? All in the same place? That sounds like the opposite of safe," Piper grumbled, mostly to themself.

"You two, stay close." Emmaline dropped her brother's arm and moved closer to Jack and Piper.

"There'll be lots of invitations to bargain," Raphael warned. He stopped walking and gestured for them to go first. "But go ahead and ask around. Stick together and say no to whatever's offered to you."

"Why would we go first?" Piper asked.

"You're the ones looking for things. Besides, I can keep an eye on who's looking at you better from behind," he said. He gave them an encouraging smile which didn't quite reach his eyes.

"Does that even make sense?" Piper muttered.

"It's gonna be okay," Emmaline said.

In a handful of steps, the path wound into the market and Piper's attention was suddenly pulled in a thousand directions. In one breath they smelt vanilla, pine, incense, sweat, bananas, the sea, and the cigarettes her grandmother had smoked.

Could that be right? They stopped and looked around, confused, letting go of Jack's arm. They hadn't smelt that smoke since Grandmother Freda had passed away, eight years ago.

A blue-skinned fey with too many eyes saw them looking and smiled. Piper couldn't easily distinguish a gender for this fey, so instantly assigned them a gender neutral pronoun. Their smile was very wide and had far too many teeth in it, ringed in like a shark's teeth. Their limbs were long and seemed to have too many elbows but something about them was intriguing. Piper half turned to move towards them but Raphael put a hand on their elbow and directed them forward.

"It's safest to talk to someone at the stalls for information rather than the randoms," he said, but not unkindly.

"Right, sorry. I just thought... thought I smelt something I knew," Piper said.

It was busier now, lots of fey milling around on and off the path. Jack eased past a group of pale fey with bright-red hair who were speaking what sounded almost like Te Reo.

Sticking together, they moved between the stalls which were set up on either side of the path. The path had started to wind and double back through the market in a kind of lazy zigzag. This maximised the number of stalls they could visit without stepping off the path.

The stalls were intriguing. Piper saw one which appeared to be run by Labrador-sized hedgehogs, selling pressed handkerchiefs and linens.

Another was stacked so high with delicious-looking fruits and vegetables that Piper couldn't see the vendor.

One stall was crowded with glass jars filled with eyeballs, ears, fingers, and other body parts. Piper was equally intrigued and repulsed.

"Are those human eyes and things?" Piper asked.

Raphael looked where they pointed and grimaced. "Yeah. Not everyone who comes over to this world knows the rules."

Jamie Sands

Jack stopped and looked at the jars, frowning. "How old are these?" She asked the small green fey behind the table. It made a gibbering noise and gestured with both hands.

Raphael moved quickly beside Jack and cleared his throat. "This isn't your concern, Detective."

"How many of the missing people in my cold cases ended up here, separated out into glass jars?" Jack hissed, turning to glare at Raphael.

"You can't save them now. Besides, if you start looking into every single one of those body parts you'll be here a century, and you'll piss off someone who can do you real harm," Raphael hissed back.

They stared into each other's eyes for a moment.

Jack swallowed, looked at the jars again, and then allowed Raphael to lead her back onto the path with the others.

Piper shuddered and reached for Emmaline's arm. Emmaline could do magic. Magic people could protect Piper.

"Maybe this one?" Emmaline said, nodding towards a grey-and-brown striped tent with an open front. A couple of squat fey with round, smiling faces and brightly coloured clothing sat behind a table, which was stacked with jars of jams, pickled things, and baked goods in handwoven baskets. They looked sort of like Hobbits, which was comforting in its familiarity.

"Worth a shot," Raphael said.

"Hi, there," Emmaline said. She tucked her hair back behind her ear.

"Hello, dear," the one in the dress replied. "Do you want to buy anything?'

"Actually, I was wondering if *Lachrimosa* meant anything to you?" She asked.

Jamie Sands

The two little fey looked at each other doubtfully. "I don't know if we know that word," the one in the dungarees said.

"Sounds like my cousin Lavinia," said the one in the dress. "Did you mean Lavinia?"

"No, definitely Lachrimosa," Jack said. "You've never heard anyone say that word?"

"I have," another voice chimed in from the other side of the path. They looked around to see a pale person whose skin was patterned with dark swirling pictures, as if he were covered with tattoos.

He wore, if it was indeed a he, tight black pants which fell just below the knees and a military-style black vest with straps over the front. The tattoos were here and there on his skin.

Piper made out a crow-looking one, and one in the form of a thorny vine on his forearm. His hair was long and dark and his eyes were a deep violet colour.

Jack stepped towards the newcomer and scowled. "And what will it cost us to hear what you know about *Lachrimosa*, mister...?"

"My name is Timaris. It's a pleasure to make your acquaintance, miss?" He bowed to her with a flourish of his hand.

"You can call me Jay," Jack said. "Nice to meet you too, Timaris." She bowed slightly at the waist, like a Japanese-style bow, her eyes staying on him.

Piper noted how polite Jack was being. Not that she was normally rude, but she was being careful with the fey. Emmaline moved up to stand by Jack's elbow and after a moment Piper took the same place on her other side.

"I'm happy to share the information with you for the smallest most insignificant of fees," Timaris said, moving closer to them.

There was a noise behind them and Piper glanced over to see Raphael had a cigarette in his mouth and was preparing to light it with his shiny silver lighter. *Fine time for it*, they thought.

Timaris's eyes flicked to Raphael and back to Jack. He'd noticed, too, and it seemed to make him nervous, judging from the way he started shifting from foot to foot.

"How small and insignificant are we talking here?" Emmaline asked.

"So small, so insignificant," Timaris said. "I only want one of your voices."

"No, we're not going to trade a voice," Jack said.

Timaris sucked his teeth and stuck his hands behind his back, rocking on his heels. "How about a selfie, then?"

"A selfie?" Piper brightened. "Sure, I can give you one of those."

"No, Pipe… Pipes," Emmaline said. Her eyes flashed a warning and she shook her head.

"Fine." Timaris looked at all of them, his eyes lingered for a moment on Raphael's lighter but his face lit up when he saw Piper's ring. "That ring, it's full of delicious sentimentality."

Piper shook their head and covered the ring with their other hand as if they could protect it by removing it from sight. "No, it was my grandmother's. Please, I need it."

"Maybe you'd consider a feeling, instead?" Emmaline said, stepping in front of Piper.

Timaris inclined his head and nodded, twisting his fingers together as if he was anticipating something wonderful. "Perhaps, if it's a particularly strong feeling, I might consider it. What kind of feeling are you offering?"

"Careful," Raphael murmured around his cigarette. The smoke from it was wafting around them all now and Piper felt comforted. Maybe because of the smell of her grandmother's smoke from earlier on, or maybe it was some magic Raphael had woven.

Jack cleared her throat. "How about love?" Emmaline looked at her, aghast. Jack was staring down Timaris, her eyes intent.

"What love?" Timaris moved closer and raised one perfect eyebrow.

"Old love, gone sour," Jack said, she brushed an invisible piece of dirt off her sleeve, taking her time in answering him.

"Love hanging around and making me stupid. How does that sound to you?"

"Sounds perfect." Timaris ran his tongue over his teeth.

"Wait, Jay. Raph – is this safe?" Emmaline asked, looking between them.

"As long as you only give him that tiny specific aspect of love, you'll be safe," Raphael said slowly. It didn't matter, though, Jack was already shaking Timaris's hand. Piper chewed on their lower lip, their heart speeding up and their chest tightening, making it harder to breathe.

28

"Information on *Lachrimosa* for your broken love," Timaris said.

"Specific information, such as what the code word means and who exactly it pertains to," Raphael cut in.

"Fine." Timaris said, his eyes were locked fast on Jack's. She met his eyes unwaveringly, although her heart was speeding up. Her skin prickled, the feeling that she was doing something dangerous flooded her with adrenaline. "I will give you specific information on *Lachirmosa*, including what it means and who it pertains to, in exchange for your broken love, if you accept these terms?"

"I accept," Jack said.

Timaris gripped her hand tight and his eyes turned from violet to slate grey. A twisting purple plume of sparkling mist appeared around their clasped hands. Jack was tempted to close her eyes, but resisted stubbornly, breathing out to release the tension so she could continue to watch. The purple mist danced about Jack, twining up her arm and around her body, teasing at her mouth which hung open ever so slightly.

From somewhere a little more distant than seemed right, Raphael inhaled sharply and spoke. "Only what was bargained for, remember, Timaris?"

Timaris scowled. The mist retracted, wound up the fey's arm and into it. As it sunk into his skin a new tattoo appeared there, coalescing as they watched. It took the form of a plant which appeared to have been freshly removed from the earth. Its roots were exposed and clumped with soil, bugs and worms dripping off it. Timaris watched, delighted.

"Ah, it's perfect!"

Jamie Sands

Jack's watched, too, fascinated as the tattoo appeared. Part of her was revolted, knowing that the image must reflect the love for Marlo which she'd just given him, but another part felt possessive of it. Timaris went to let go of her hand and she let go almost reluctantly, aware that now the feeling was transferred, she was letting go of something much larger.

She heard Emmaline's voice vaguely. "What else did he try to take?"

"The information you owe us, Timaris?" Raphael prompted.

"Easy, you're after the Wild Hunt, yeah? I'm a member. What did you want to know? You got someone to kidnap?" Timaris stroked a finger around his new tattoo, clearly besotted.

"No!" Piper said, shocked. It was a bit loud. Jack looked over at them, surprised. Their cheeks flamed and they stepped back a bit, closer to Raphael, and pressed their lips together. Jack refocused on the job at hand and turned back to Timaris.

"No, we're looking for someone who may have been a victim of yours, her name is Edith," Jack said.

"I have her picture," Piper said. They pulled a print out of their pocket and handed it to Jack, who showed it to Timaris.

"Hmm." He tilted his head this way and that, squinted his eyes, and nodded. "Yes. We did her. Stole her away, as requested."

"Good. Where did you take her?" Jack's patience was wearing thin, she felt like she was interviewing a difficult witness and needed to be a bit more persuasive to get the information out.

"We didn't stipulate exactly how much I'd tell you," he said. His voice took on a wheedling quality. "Something more for something more."

"Don't. You said my feelings were perfect." Jack, annoyance bubbling inside her, prodded the plant tattoo on his bicep and he flinched as if it had been freshly inked with a tattooist's needle. "Tell me what you know."

"Fine. We did it and we delivered her where we were meant to. We were paid and we did the job, what happens after is nothing to do with us."

Jack's patience snapped and she grabbed a handful of the elegant black vest Timaris was wearing and yanked him up and towards her. He was as light as a child.

"Where did you take her?" Jack said through gritted teeth. Raphael made a surprised noise and moved closer, but he didn't interfere.

"We took her to the centre of the Withering Woods. The woman who paid us, she was there waiting. She never gave us her name," Timaris said.

"Good. See how easy talking is? What did she look like?" Jack snarled.

"Like a mage, one of them." He nodded at Emmaline and Raphael, his hands scrabbled on Jack's wrist, scratching her lightly, but she didn't let go of him. "Had that smell about her."

"A mage. And her hair, what colour was it? How about her skin; was it pale like mine or darker like my friend's? Any information at all about her appearance?"

"Long hair, black and purple. Pale skin. Looked like she belonged with the dark fey."

"Was her name Aeva?" Piper asked, moving closer.

Timaris looked over at Piper, letting his hands fall to his sides. "She never gave us a name. It could have been that. Or it could have been anything else at all."

"Aeva?" Jack put Timaris down and he adjusted his clothing. "Edith's neighbour?"

"She said she was in a Wiccan group, maybe it was her cover for being a mage?" Piper shrugged. "Valerie knew her, remember?"

"Did you kill David Andrews?" Jack asked. It was almost an afterthought, but since she'd managed to intimidate Timaris, she might as well milk it.

"Who's David Andrews?" Emmaline whispered to Piper.

"One of her old cases, never solved," Piper whispered back.

"We've killed many," Timaris said. "In the old days, mortals would quake and quail when we rode, our hounds baying. They'd lock themselves in their houses and pray we passed them by."

Jack growled in frustration and turned to Raphael. "I want to arrest all of them. All. Of. Them."

"You can't." Jack looked Raphael in the eyes, about to argue, but there was something in them that Jack didn't want to contradict. A hardness to the soft blue which she hadn't noticed before. She remembered what Emmaline had said about Raphael's powers and how he was their expert in this place. She looked away and breathed out heavily. "The fairy kind are not subject to human laws. You don't have jurisdiction," he said.

"And they want to trade in selfies?" Piper asked, laughing a little.

"We have to move with the times," the fey said. He flicked his hair back over his shoulder. "No one's heard of us anymore, so they don't fear us. Selfies are valuable." He licked his lips.

Jack whirled to Timaris and jabbed a finger at him, feeling quite satisfied when he took a half step back from her.

"Fine. This was useful. Don't kill any more people, or I'm coming back and I don't care about jurisdiction." Jack turned away from him towards Raphael and the others.

Timaris put a hand on her elbow, which startled her.

"Anytime you want to trade again, I'll be keen. Your feelings are delicious, delectable, satisfying," he eyed her. "I felt some others... very interesting variations and agonies, when I took your love."

"I'll bear it in mind," Jack said. She shook her arm loose from his grip. Raphael gestured back up the path.

"All right, let's get out of here before something else happens."

They went quickly back towards the path to Gerard's house. Jack striding ahead, Piper hurrying to keep up, and to keep in between Jack and Raphael in the marching order. Emmaline walked alongside Piper, watching Jack's back with concern.

29

Gerard's house was as fairy-tale perfect on the inside as it was on the outside. The kitchen had a proper hearth with a cast-iron kettle on a hook over the fire. The living room was lined with sofas and shelves. The sofas were stacked with cushions and blankets, the shelves were full of books and strange mementoes. Emmaline and Jack were in the lounge, waiting for Piper to bring in tea.

"That was amazing, how you handled Timaris," Emmaline said.

"Was it? Just doing my job," Jack said, she fought a smile for a moment, then decided there was no point fighting it. "And it worked, we got a name. We have a lead. I hated walking away from a mass murderer, though."

"How do you feel? After he did magic on you?"

"I don't know, the same? I suppose I feel lighter, freer, maybe." Jack shrugged and leaned back against the couch's arm. The whole day had been a whirlwind and she wanted a rest. This was nice, but it wasn't lying down and sleeping.

"Whatever happened, you were amazing. So strong. I really admire that about you."

Jack looked at Emmaline for a moment and half turned so she was facing her. Something Emmaline had just said had frightened her. She'd been flirting with her off and on, and Jack hadn't hated it, had even flirted back a little. But she had to put a stop to things before Emmaline got too attached.

"Look, Em. I really appreciate that you've been so much help. I mean, we literally couldn't have got this far on the case without you, so – big help. And the way you've assisted me and Piper to understand what's going on, showing us, all this, the magic and everything. So grateful. Words can't express

how much." Jack swallowed.

"But?" Emmaline prompted, her eyes wide and wary.

"But our relationship can't be any more than this, work

acquaintances."

"Not even friends?" Emmaline folded her arms, closing

herself off from Jack, building a wall. Jack had seen it a

million times when people didn't want to accept what was

going on. At least she wasn't telling Emmaline that her

brother was dead, or something.

This was for the best, Jack told herself. It's better, kinder, to

hurt her a little now, before it was more than a crush. They'd

only known each other a couple of days. Jack didn't believe in

love at first sight.

"I'm sorry. I'm not good at any of this. Love, friends, human

relationships. I'm a train wreck. I don't want you to go getting attached and then be disappointed," Jack said, quickly, trying to put the blame on herself and not allow Emmaline to feel too hurt.

"I, uh, sure. I thought there was a bit of a vibe between us, but. It's fine. I understand," Emmaline said. Her voice was harder, defensive.

"Thanks," Jack said. She should feel relieved. Emmaline had agreed with her, had said the perfect thing.

Instead, her stomach sank, like she'd taken a step but the ground underneath her foot was further away than she'd expected. An uncomfortable jolt.

Em stood up and went into the kitchen, walking quickly, her arms folded tight.

There was silence in the living room. Jack breathed out slowly, trying to loosen the tension in her chest.

30

"Well, that was interesting," a dry voice said from the corner of the room. Jack saw a dark, horned figure lounging with one shoulder against the doorframe.

"Gerard, right?" Jack shifted in her seat. The man had looked wan but human over the mirror – over magical facetime. But that was not the man standing before her now.

Gerard's eyes were shiny and obsidian, short black horns pushed out of his forehead and added a distinct air of menace about him.

He had a dangerous vibe. He looked like the bad-boy hero of a teenage paranormal romance movie. He caught her gaze and his hand went up to his horns. His demeanour changed from bad boy to concern, a much more human expression.

Jamie Sands

"I'm sorry. I can change back if it would make you more comfortable?" he said.

"It's fine," she said. She shook off the uncomfortable feeling. "I'm Jack."

"I remember talking to you through the mirror, Detective." He sat in one of the armchairs across from her. "Em really likes you, you know."

"I had an inkling," Jack said dryly.

"Why don't you indulge the inkling? I don't think you dislike her." He scratched at the worn upholstery of the armchair with one talon-like nail.

"I don't have time for a relationship," Jack said. Something about the candid way Gerard had spoken encouraged her to do the same, even though she barely knew him.

"When will you have time? I don't get aromantic or asexual feelings from you."

"Aromatic?" Jack's eyebrows pulled together.

"Uninterested in love or romance, aromantic." He put emphasis on the 'man' part of the word.

"Would you be able to... feel that? If I was?" Jack was aware this was the kind of situation that she'd usually count as crossing boundaries, but fuck it. They were in another universe. She was talking to a boy with horns. A man. A changeling – whatever he was.

"Yes, I'm dark fey, my kind, well we feed on human emotions. Besides, I've been trained, err, educated by an incubus and a kelpie. I've learnt how to taste various predilections and desires." He smiled and his teeth seemed a little more pointy than they should have been.

"What's an incubus and a kelpie?" Jack asked. Anything to not think about the feeding off emotions stuff he'd said.

"Incubus and succubus are fey who... well, in legends and folklore, humans thought were demons. They use the sexual arts to feed. They like the taste of lust and desire, that kind of thing."

"Succubus does sound familiar." Jack crossed her legs. Gerard's voice was silky smooth. It was the same voice that had stuttered and been uncertain earlier. But now, it was charged with confidence and sexual energy. She wasn't attracted to him, but she felt like this usually worked on people. Like if they kept talking long enough, she might... start to be attracted to him?

That was somewhat unsettling. Jack had been gay her entire life. She shook her head and discarded the thought.

"The first recording of a succubus interfering with a human dates back to Mesopotamia," Gerard said. He suddenly sounded less like he was trying to seduce her and more like an academic lecturing on something he thought was fascinating.

"Okay, and the other one?"

"Kelpies are shapeshifters, mostly from around the Scottish waterways. They're also very seductive. They appear like a beautiful person, or a handsome horse, and lure people to their deaths." He licked his lips. "So like I say, I've had experience with sex magic and recognising predilections."

"Must make you a blast at parties," Jack joked. She was trying to defuse the tension building in the room. Although she knew Raphael trusted Gerard, she was starting to feel less than comfortable.

"More than you think." He smiled, showing off his pointed teeth again. Jack stiffened and glanced towards the door, wondering what would happen if she ran for it.

Emmaline, Piper, and Raphael bustled in with cups of tea, a couple of plates of cookies, stacks of toast, and fresh chopped vegetables.

That broke the tension. Jack breathed out.

"Ger, you're not being weird and dark at Jack, are you? She's new to all this," Raphael said, ruffling Gerard's hair affectionately.

"Shit, I actually might be." Gerard closed his eyes and the horns retracted into his head. When he opened his eyes, they were a deep, clear blue with a black pupil: human eyes. Jack breathed easier.

"He sometimes forgets," Raphael said. He sat beside Jack and offered her a cup of tea, which she accepted gratefully. It felt like they'd been having hot drinks all day but this one she really wanted to steady her nerves.

"It's hard when I've been seeing so much of Farren," Gerard said. He wrapped his hands around a steaming mug and looked directly into Jack's eyes. "I'm sorry, Jack, I really am. I never used to be like this, but when I went fey everything changed, pretty literally. Is that marmalade?"

"Of course it is, Lina brought it back the last time she went over," Raphael said. "Just for you because literally no one else in the world likes marmalade."

"More for me." Gerard spread a slice of toast with a generous amount of marmalade and started munching. He offered the plate of toast to Jack, but she shook her head.

"This food is safe, right?" Piper asked. They picked up a cookie and examined it.

Jamie Sands

"Yes, this is all from Earth. We bring it over to stock the house," Gerard said. "Nothing fey about it."

"Where is she? Uh, Lina, I mean," Emmaline asked, looking around as if she might appear.

Maybe *she would,* Jack thought. It seemed like anything might happen here. Jack's eyes wandered to the window, half expecting something to pop up there, an eerie face, or a hand scratching at the window. This place was unpredictable, there was no way to get used to it.

"She took her apprentice to the Glades," Gerard said around a mouthful of toast. "I dunno when she'll be back."

"She's such a good teacher, I don't know why she's never taken an apprentice before," Raphael said.

"She didn't have the confidence," Emmaline said. "Now she does."

Piper, who'd settled on the armchair closest to Jack, leaned on their knee to get closer to her and stage whispered. "Any idea who they're talking about?" Piper asked.

"Raphael said the house was Gerard and Lina's, maybe they're married?"

"Siblings," Raphael said, overhearing them. "Twins."

"So, you found what you wanted?" Gerard asked.

"Yeah, I think so. Now we have someone to talk to back on the other side," Emmaline said, into her cup of tea.

"Two people," Piper said. "Aeva du Maurier and Abel Armstrong."

"Right," Emmaline grumbled. "I guess you'll only want my help with Aeva."

"You're on this case now," said Jack, quickly. "We'll want your help on everything." Emmaline gave her a tight smile which could have been gratitude but could've been awkwardness, as well. Probably, it was both.

Jack caught the sound of movement from upstairs and looked up at the ceiling, her heart racing and her imagination supplying images of weird fey invading the building to kill them all. "What was that?"

"Oh, Amy's awake," Raphael said. His face took on a soft, gooey smile. Jack heard Piper sigh and sit back.

"Are you all right?" Jack asked Piper.

"Yes, fine. He's just so handsome," Piper murmured.

The thumps moved about, then Amy came downstairs. She was petite, but not as small as Emmaline. It was clear she was in top physical condition. Jack thought ex-military or police, based on her upright posture and obviously toned arms. She was wearing a man's grey T-shirt with a Fall Out

Boy logo on it and yoga pants, her long ash-blonde hair pulled back in a messy bun.

"Wow, okay, lots of people," she said. She stopped in the doorway to survey the room, one of her hands crossing her chest to hold on to her other arm. Raphael went to her side, putting his hand in hers and speaking in a soothing tone.

"Emmaline brought Jack and Piper over from the human world. She's helping them out. They're cops, normal humans. They're researching a case and this is their first time in Faerie," Raphael said.

"I'm Jack," Jack said. She raised her hand to wave at Amy.

"It's good to meet you," Amy said, her voice bland, almost automatic. Then she turned to Emmaline and beamed. "And you're Raphael's little sister?"

Jack sat back in the sofa, starting to feel sleepy now that the attention was off her. Raphael and Amy crossed the room and sat side by side on the couch. As they moved, Jack caught sight of a strangely shaped scar on the inside of Amy's wrist. She waited for a lull in the conversation and cleared her throat.

"Amy, what's the mark on the inside of your wrist?" Jack asked.

Amy looked at her wrist and held it out to Jack so she could see it. "It's the mark of my, uh, the cult I used to be in, the Order of Mage Hunters."

"Mage hunters." Jack blinked and examined the mark. It looked like a brand. The skin was shiny and raised even though it was old, scarred skin. It was a circular symbol with a sort of spiral in the middle, except it was more complicated than that.

"Amy and I met because she was meant to kill me." Raphael said brightly, his eyes sparkling.

"You're the only one who thinks it's funny, love,' Amy said. She kissed his cheek.

"I think it's hilarious," he said.

"You were supposed to kill him?" Piper repeated.

"It's true. Mage hunters are this horrible secret cult who train people to track down magic-users and then kill them. They think we're all evil," Raphael said, slipping his arm around Amy's shoulders and pulling her closer in. "It's like a religious order, very zealous and intense."

"To be fair, some of you are evil," Amy said, nudging him in the ribs with her elbow.

"Right, but the Order of Mage Hunters is way more evil," Emmaline said. "But it's okay, because Raph turned Amy good with the power of his love."

"That makes me sound way more heroic than I was," Raphael said, laughing. "I mostly annoyed her with logic and wouldn't shut up until she saw things from another point of view."

"Whatever happened, I'm not one of them anymore," Amy said, she smiled at Jack as if willing her to believe it. Jack half smiled back, but this all felt like more information on a mission which had already scrambled her brain somewhat.

Piper yawned and Jack glanced at them, hoping this was a good cue to excuse themselves from Gerard and company.

"You tired?" Jack asked. "We don't have to be here any longer, we just need someone to get us back through."

"Oh, of course, you must be tired. I'll take you back through," Raphael said, letting go of Amy.

"It was lovely to meet you in person," Gerard said.

Jack smiled and shook his hand and hoped he couldn't tell that she was still a little unsettled by him. "Thanks for your hospitality. Good luck with... everything. Nice to meet you, Amy." She took Piper by the elbow and steered them towards Raphael.

She'd be able to relax once they were back on the right side of the mirror.

31

Raphael did the incantation to get them back to the other side of the mirror.

When they came through, it was the middle of the night. Piper's phone had been freaking out the entire time they were in Faerie. It'd been saying 'searching for signal', and then displayed some weird characters, and turned itself to flight mode. When Piper'd turned flight mode off, it'd done the same again. And the battery was hugely drained. They'd decided it was safer just to leave it how it wanted to be and pocket it.

Back in Raphael's apartment, Piper looked out the window to confirm the landscape was Auckland and switched their phone off flight mode again. After a moment, it had the network signal and the display looked a bit more normal.

"It's thirteen minutes past one," Piper said. "But, we went through at like, ten-thirty, and it felt like we were there for the whole night."

"Time's weird over there," Emmaline said. She patted Piper on the shoulder.

"All good? I'll be off again," Raphael said. His head, shoulders, and torso were poking through the mirror. He hadn't walked all the way through the portal. It was a weird thing to look at, and Piper's head began to hurt. "Lovely to meet you two, and see you again soon, Em."

"Night, Raph," Emmaline leaned in and kissed his cheek. "Love you."

"Love you too, baby sister. Check in on Max if you get a chance, will you? I'm sure he'd love to hear from you." He waved at the others and vanished back into the smooth surface of the mirror.

"Will do." Emmaline watched the portal close before she yawned, stretching her arms up over her head. Piper noticed Jack watching her, saw the way her eyes wandered to the strip of skin revealed when Emmaline's shirt rode up.

"Right, well, thanks for everything. We'd better get going." Jack said suddenly, turning away and fishing in her pockets for her keys. "Do you need a lift home, Emmaline?"

"No, it's fine. I'll catch an Uber."

Piper looked between them. Where was this coldness coming from? Jack had asked the question as if it were a duty. Emmaline had been quick to turn down the ride. Piper'd missed something.

"What time in the morning are we getting started?" Piper asked.

"Let's sleep in," Jack said. She yawned as if even the idea of sleep was enough to make the day catch up with her. Or maybe it was a contagious yawn from Emmaline?

"Eight-thirty or nine?" Piper asked. They could ask this in the car, obviously, but they wanted to make sure Emmaline was in the loop. Something had happened while Piper was making tea, and they didn't know what it was. Whatever had happened, Piper was determined that no weirdness was going to get in the way.

"Sure, nine sounds good," Jack said. "Abel or Aeva first, do you think?"

"Aeva," Piper said. "We know she was directly involved."

"Makes sense," Emmaline said.

"Sorted," Jack said. She spun the keys on her finger and led the way out onto the street. "See you tomorrow, Emmaline."

32

Jack woke to the sound of knocking on her door. It was loud. Much louder than it should have been. And it was a hollow-sounding knock, not like the solid knock of the front door. If someone had sneaked in to attack her, why would they knock on the door?

Her instincts kicked in – this could be a threat.

She sat up, grabbed the baseball bat she kept behind her nightstand, and got out of bed.

"Who's there? I'm armed."

"It's Emmaline, please don't shoot at me." Emmaline's voice called from the other side of the door. Jack went to the bedroom door and opened it. She flicked on the hallway light.

Emmaline stood in the hallway, looking like a drowned rat. Her blonde hair was plastered to her head and her eyes looked gigantic. She wore purple pyjamas with little black bats on them, and these were also soaked and clinging to her. Jack became vaguely aware of the rain outside, but that was hardly the biggest problem right now.

"Are you inside my house?" Jack blinked, looking past Emmaline as if the explanation would be there.

"Yes, sorry. I let myself in the front door, I was scared. I locked it again when I was inside. I'm sorry to barge in on you, but I was attacked. I had to get away." Emmaline wrapped her arms around herself, and Jack felt her own heart flutter with sympathy and a thrill of fear.

"Attacked?" Jack propped the baseball bat against the wall.

"Shit. Are you okay?'

"Um?" Emmaline rubbed her hand over her eyes. "Not really. They got into my place and I freaked and bailed. I came here because... Because I thought you'd be the best protection, and you're not like, a mage. so you're not known to them."

"To them?"

"Mage hunters," Emmaline said, her voice quivering a bit. "I don't know how they found me, maybe it was just a lucky..." she shook her head and wiped her eyes again. "I've never actually had to fight them before."

The air shot out of Jack's lungs as she imagined what could have happened. Emmaline could have died – that's what Raphael and Amy had said the hunters did.

"Mage hunters? Like Amy was?" Jack took Emmaline by the elbow and led her into the living room. "Are you hurt at all? What happened?"

"No, I'm not hurt. I brought up a crocodile spirit to distract them and escaped out the back door. It was freaky, I don't know how they found me. I hitchhiked over the bridge and walked a couple blocks and it started raining and I had to magic your locks open. They're secure again now, and I put some extra protection on the door." Emmaline sniffed hard, pushed her hair back from her forehead, and paused. She looked Jack up and down. "Are those dinosaur pyjamas?"

"The shorts of them," Jack said. She slept in an old police training college T-shirt, but regular pyjama pants. "How about you jump in the shower to warm up and I'll find you something dry to wear?"

"Perfect. Thanks, Jack," Emmaline said, she attempted a smile but it was clearly a strain, her face was so pale it was almost translucent. Jack felt a surge of protectiveness. "I'm sorry to wake you up like this."

"Don't worry. It's fine that you came here, don't apologise."

Jack wanted to hug Emmaline, but after their talk earlier, she didn't think it'd be welcome. Instead, she went to the kitchen and pulled out her bottle of Scotch. "Here, for your nerves." She poured out a dram and handed it to Emmaline, who'd followed her. Emmaline downed it in one, shivered, and held the empty glass out to Jack.

"More, please." Jack smiled softly, then obliged with a generous helping which Emmaline drank it marginally slower. "Thanks. Shower?"

"It's through here." Jack led her to the bathroom. "The towels on the shelf are clean. Take your time."

She closed the door behind Emmaline and went to check on the front door. She'd put the bolt and chain on before going to bed, she knew she had. How had Emmaline managed to get inside? She'd magicked the door? What did that even mean?

Should Jack be barring her door with magic now? Had Emmaline already done that?

Jack shook her head and took a breath to refocus. None of this was the biggest issue right now. The biggest issue was that Emmaline was in her house, and she needed taking care of.

Jack returned her baseball bat to its spot behind the side table in her bedroom and dug out some clean workout gear. She piled up soft grey trackpants, a T-shirt, thick socks, and a hoodie which would fit Emmaline without swamping her. She set them down on the floor outside the bathroom door then went into the kitchen to put on the kettle, pulling a hot-water bottle out of the bottom drawer.

There was nothing more comforting than a hot-water bottle when you'd had a shock.

She'd finished filling it up and was wrapping it in a tea towel when Emmaline came into the kitchen, towelling her hair dry. She looked objectively adorable wearing Jack's workout gear. Jack felt her cheeks warm and turned away to pretend she was refastening the bottle.

"Really, I'm sorry about this." Emmaline said, hesitancy making her voice quiver. "I know you said all that stuff about being business acquaintances and it's super uncool of me to turn up at four in the morning, but I just…" she trailed off, which Jack was glad for. She wasn't sure she was ready for Emmaline's reasons.

"It's all right." Jack turned back to Emmaline so she could see Jack meant it. "Like you said, it's a good bet they wouldn't think to come here. Should I do anything, uh, extra, to the door?"

"I put some wards up on it as soon as I got inside. I hope you're okay with that."

"No, that's fine. You might want to do the window over there, too? I leave it open for this stray cat to come in." Jack nodded at the window and then handed her the hot-water bottle. "For you, I thought it might help."

Emmaline wrapped her arms around the hot-water bottle and hummed with pleasure. "Thank you, it does help."

"So, these people who came into your place," Jack said. "Are you okay to talk about it?"

Emmaline nodded, and pressed her lips together, looking haunted. "Let's sit, though?"

They settled on the couch, facing each other. Jack wished for her phone to record what Emmaline said, but she supposed this wasn't like a random witness. She could always ask Emmaline again.

Jamie Sands

"Okay, so. Did you recognise any of them?"

Emmaline shook her head. "No, they were all strangers. I knew where they were from, though, with those weird black tactical suits they wear. I knew I had to get out. I was surprised they'd sent three people – usually they'd just send one. Maybe's it's because they know I'm a..." she trailed off and looked at Jack apologetically. "I guess I've never actually told you what kind of magic I do."

There were three of them, Jack made a mental note and raised her eyebrows. "No, you haven't. Something about spirits is really all I've picked up."

"I'm a necromancer," Emmaline said. She didn't sound enthusiastic about telling Jack this. Jack had heard the word before, images of black magic – cults sacrificing innocents and the like – sprung to mind. None of those images matched with what she knew of sweet, gentle Emmaline.

"I might need you to explain that a bit more, if you don't mind." Jack poured them both another shot of whiskey and downed hers in one. Emmaline eyed hers and set it on the coffee table again.

"Well, I deal with death magic. But it's not what it sounds like, truly. I don't raise the dead or create zombies or anything like that, I mostly talk to the spirits of those who have passed. I can store life essence and so on, and bind spirits to help me, but it's not... I'm not evil," she finished, a little weakly.

"I know you're not evil," Jack said, surprising herself with how much she meant it. Emmaline smiled a bit. "I don't know that I entirely understand, though. You said something about a crocodile earlier?"

"Right, an old crocodile spirit from Northern Australia. I bound it just in case I was ever attacked, and it seemed like a good time."

"So it can hurt people, even though it's, what, a ghost?"

Emmaline picked up the whiskey and downed it before she nodded. "Yeah, basically. Imagine I took a ghost and then gave it enough power that it could bite people, and that's more or less it."

Jack sat back, let that new bit of knowledge settle into her brain, and sighed. "Yeah, all right. I think I get it. So, you didn't recognise any of the attackers. Would you recognise them if you saw them again?"

Emmaline nodded. "Oh, yeah. I could give you descriptions."

"That'd be great. I can't help but wonder if they're linked to this case somehow. Are you sure they were hunters and not the, y'know, fey Wild Hunt?"

"Oh yeah, definitely." Emmaline pulled her knees up to her chest, pressing the hot-water bottle to her. "I can sense glamour and these guys had none, they were the real thing."

"Do you know how they got into your place?"

"Broke a window, I think, but I didn't really stick around to check it out." Emmaline rested her chin on her knees and huffed out her breath. She looked tired and sad and Jack suddenly felt like a bully for asking all these questions.

They could go over it again in the morning. "Right, let's, uh. Get some sleep. Where'd you put your wet pyjamas?"

"They're on the floor of the bathroom?"

"I'll put them in the wash." Jack got up to collect the wet clothes, bringing them back into the kitchen, she put them into the washing machine.

"You're a bit of a neat freak, huh?" Emmaline leaned on the counter, hugging the hot-water bottle to her chest. She was carrying it around like a teddy bear, which – again – was damn adorable.

"Yeah. I guess I always had to be neat as a kid, and I'm used to it, now."

"Right, so. I can take the couch as long as there's a blanket," Emmaline said. "We said we'd meet Piper at nine, and that's only a few hours away."

"Take the bed," Jack said. She hadn't meant to say that, exactly, but it felt right to offer her the bed. She'd gone through a nasty experience, being attacked in her house, and Jack wanted her to have some comfort and get some good rest. She also half wanted to climb in next to her, hold her, and tell her it was going to be all right, but she wasn't about to admit that.

"No! Don't be silly, I barged in on you, you shouldn't give up your bed."

"You woke me up, it'll take me some time to get back to sleep. So you take the bed. I'll watch TV until I fall asleep. You rest up. You must be freaked," Jack said.

Em opened her mouth to argue but closed it again before nodding. "Thanks, Jack. And thanks for this," she held up the hot-water bottle, turned and went into Jack's room.

Once the door was closed, Jack's mind raced with a hundred possible things she could do. She could phone Piper and let them know what had happened. She could go and hold Emmaline. She could log the attack with the station, she could go over all the case notes and try and find a link between Edith's disappearance and hunters ambushing Emmaline in the middle of the night.

But Jack did none of those things. Instead, she recorded what Emmaline had told her onto a notepad, making a mental note to put it on her phone the next day. She turned off lights, retrieved her sleeping bag and spare pillow from the hall cupboard, and went into the living room.

There, she set herself up on the couch and switched the TV to static and turned the sound down low. It wouldn't take long for her to drop off, even with all the questions hovering over her. They could wait. Besides, she could answer them better if she was rested.

33

Jack woke up at sunrise, as the first beams of light came through the window directly into her face.

It took her a moment to remember why she was sleeping out on the couch, and then she remembered Emmaline turning up in the middle of the night looking for help.

Her neck complained about the angle of her head, propped on a cushion on the couch. She sat up to try and stretch it out, but it didn't seem to help. She tried another position but she was too sore.

She wondered if she should go for a run, but she looked at the bedroom door. Her workout clothes were on Emmaline. Her other workout clothes were in her bedroom. And Emmaline was in her bed. And Jack's cell phone was also charging in the bedroom.

Jamie Sands

Of course, it was her house, she could go in there. She could move quietly through the room and pick up some clothes and her cell phone.

Technically she *could*.

But it would feel so much like invading Emmaline's privacy, which she definitely didn't want to do after such a horrible night. It wouldn't help her relax or feel safe or comfortable.

And there was the whole 'startled mage' thing, where if Jack went in there and Emmaline saw it as a sign of attack, she might throw some magic at Jack. And who could say what that would look like?

Jack sighed, punched the pillow until it was vaguely comfortable, and dropped back into a fitful sleep.

She woke up to Emmaline shaking her shoulder. Jack looked up to see Emmaline with her hair tousled from sleep, looking grumpy. There was a weird noise. Emmaline shoved Jack's phone at her.

"It's ringing."

Right, the weird noise. Jack's phone. She took the phone and flipped it open. "This is Jack."

"Jack, it's Omid, at the station. We got a missing person. Thought you'd like to know, since you talked to this guy for your case."

"Omid, what's happening?" Jack said. She sat up, her heart racing from the abrupt wake-up call and her mind snapping to attention at his words.

"The reverend, uh... Zebedee? He's gone missing," Omid said.

"What?!"

Em raised her eyebrows and went to the kitchen.

Jamie Sands

"The reverend, he was taken from the church last night."

"Fuck. Were there witnesses?" Jack rubbed the sleep out of her eyes and pushed her way out of the sleeping bag.

"Mm-hm, the choir was practising. He was there and then suddenly he wasn't." She heard the sound of typing. "It's super weird, just like the things you love."

"Shit, shit, shit. This was last night?" Jack sat up, taking a moment to untangle her legs from the sleeping bag before shoving it aside.

"Yeah. It took ages to get all the stories and connect the dots. Would've called you sooner, but figured we may as well interview everyone first."

"I'll be in soon to look over the report. Thanks, Omid. This is directly connected to my case." Jack hung up and stood up, swearing to herself.

"Hey grumpy bear, where do you keep the coffee?" Emmaline asked.

"Pantry, it's the door beside the fridge. I'm taking a shower, fast. We need to get going."

"Get going?" Emmaline asked. "What was the call about?"

"The rev's disappeared, possibly in front of people," Jack said. She paused at the door to the kitchen. "Can't tell if this is breaking the case open or making it worse, but either way, it's something."

34

Piper, fuming, slammed the door to the car and took their seat in the back with their arms folded, glaring daggers at Jack. "You said we'd be sleeping in today. You said nine."

"I know, but I got a call from the station. Our case just got way more complicated."

"Sorry, Piper." Emmaline turned in the passenger seat and frowned at Piper. "How about we get doughnuts on the way? My shout."

"Doughnuts would help," Piper said. They gave Emmaline a small smile.

"Even though it's a horrible stereotype?" Jack asked.

"Doughnuts," Piper nodded. "I want a great big chocolatey drink and a doughnut with pink frosting and sprinkles."

"Coming up," Jack said.

Piper looked between them. Jack and Emmaline were getting on well again. And they were both in the car before Piper. And Emmaline was wearing an outfit that looked like it could've been assembled from Jack's wardrobe. What the hell was going on?

"So, you two were together this morning?" Piper asked.

"I was attacked in the night," Emmaline said. "Mage hunters. I didn't even know mage hunters had made it to New Zealand. But there they were."

"Shit, I'm sorry," Piper said. "Were you hurt?"

"No, I got away and went to Jack's place," Emmaline said. "I'm fine."

"How did you know where Jack lives?" Piper asked. Jack glanced at Emmaline, like she hadn't thought of that herself.

"I used a tracking spell," Emmaline said. "When I know someone's name I can track them, if I have something of theirs. Like I tried to do with Edith right when we first met."

"You have something of mine?" Jack asked.

"The cup you drank tea from," Emmaline said. "I hadn't done the dishes yet so it had your saliva on it still."

"Ew," Piper said.

"And that's another good reason to always do your dishes right away," Jack murmured. She pulled into the Dunkin' Donuts and they piled out to choose something for breakfast.

"Please state your name," Jack said. She pressed 'record' on her phone.

They had gathered the choir back in the church to get their statements, and the atmosphere was almost like a party.

Jack, Piper, and a few other officers were taking statements quickly, letting people know they could leave once they'd given theirs, but many were sticking around to help out in any way they could.

The reason for the summons was serious, but these were all such happy, friendly people so comfortable with each other that the building was filled with chatter. Some had even brought food, there was a big tray of pikelets with jam and cream being passed around.

Jack had taken to bringing her witnesses into the corner, a bit out of the way of the main noise. They sat on padded office chairs, facing each other. Jack balanced her phone on one knee and held her notepad in her hand.

"Arabella Ann," the old lady said. "Arabella Ann Gold."

"Hi, Arabella. How long have you been singing in this church's choir?"

Jamie Sands

"Eight years, dear," Arabella said. "I started when I moved up here to be nearer to my grandchildren."

"So, you were singing?" Jack asked. She tried to give Arabella a smile the way Piper seemed to know how to do without thinking about it.

Arabella didn't seem particularly comforted by Jack's efforts. She raised her eyebrows and rubbed her hands together as if she was cold.

"That's right. We were practising 'Abide With Me'," Arabella said. "It was our second time through, because some of the younger ones hadn't been paying too much attention. It's such a lovely song, don't you think?"

"I'm sure it is," Jack said. She leaned back in her chair. "Can you please describe what happened to the reverend?"

"It was the strangest thing," Arabella said. "I thought maybe I'd had a stroke for a moment; he was there and then he wasn't. If it hadn't been for Hisako I'm sure I'd have been on the floor."

"Hisako?" Jack asked. She checked the list of choir members and saw his name there.

"He stands beside me," Arabella said. She looked past Jack to the crowd and pointed him out to her. "There, see? He has very strong arms."

"Right, thanks. So the reverend was there and then he wasn't," Jack made a note. "Can you describe that a little more?"

"He was at the front, directing, like he always does. But in between two words, he was gone – like he'd never been there. Not even a footprint on the floor." Arabella flung her hands out to each side and made a *huh* sound to emphasise the point.

Jamie Sands

Jack tried to imagine someone vanishing directly in front of her and couldn't, even after all the business with going through the mirror. "It must've been horrible. And the others saw this as well? What happened next?"

"Graham went to check out the back, in case Zebedee was playing a trick on us." Arabella started to count on her fingers. "Then Mavis called the police. A couple of the younger ones thought maybe it was the rapture and he'd ascended." Arabella shook her head. "Ridiculous."

"What do you think happened?"

"I'm sure I don't know. Maybe the aliens took him? I've seen some documentaries about that on Netflix, you know. It happens a lot more than people think it does." She'd leaned forward as if she was sharing a conspiracy theory. Maybe all the alien abduction cases in the world were just fairies stealing people? That opened up a whole can of worms, one that Jack didn't have time to consider.

"That's certainly an option." She made a couple of notes and picked up her phone to turn the recording off. "This has been very helpful, thank you, Arabella."

"Will you be able to find him?" Arabella asked. Jack looked into her wrinkled face, which was shining with hope and trust, her eyes clear and piercing.

"We're going to try," Jack said. It didn't quite feel like enough, so she tried again. "We're going to do our absolute best to find him and bring him back. If you think of anything else, please let us know." She handed Arabella her card and smiled again.

"Of course, dear," Arabella said.

Jack went over to Piper, who was talking with a man of about sixty. The two of them were laughing like old friends, and

Jamie Sands

Jack watched, a little in awe. How did Piper have such an easy way with everyone? It seemed like a natural gift, and Jack felt envious.

Piper saw Jack watching and thanked the man, clasping his hand with both of theirs. He nodded and promised to call them if he heard any news.

Piper got up and showed Jack the notes. "That's the fifth one I've spoken with and they all say the same thing. The reverend just vanished while they were singing, now you see him, now you don't."

"Same as mine," Jack said. "How about we finish up with the rest of the choir and compare all the data points?"

"Sounds fun," Piper said. They seemed to mean it, too.

"How do you do it?" Jack said. But she said it under her breath, once Piper had turned to go and speak to the next member of the choir, so Piper didn't hear her.

35

"All of these stories match up," Piper said and sighed, because if everyone agreed, that meant they didn't have anything to go on except magic.

They were back at the station, sifting through statements and comparing notes. Piper was using half of Jack's desk, Jack had moved her things over to give her space. Emmaline sat nearby, reading a paperback novel she'd found in the waiting room.

"Which means halfway through choir rehearsal last night, in between the second and third verses of 'Abide With Me', the whole choir blinked and the reverend vanished. He was there leading them until he was gone," Jack said. She rubbed her forehead in between her eyebrows.

"Had to be magic," Emmaline said, closing the paperback and setting it on the edge of Jack's desk. "I'm not sure what spell it was, or who would do something so obvious in front of so many people. And in a church, it's totally poor taste, n'est-ce pas? Guache."

"Poor taste doesn't even cover it," Piper said, sighing. "There were some really old people in the choir and they're freaked out. One had to go to hospital because they were having heart palpitations."

"Could Aeva have done this?" Jack asked.

"I mean, maybe. I really don't know what type of mage she is or what she can do, but it's possible," Emmaline said.

"We should go talk to her, right?" Piper said. They dusted their hands off, having just finished off their third doughnut.

"Yeah, we should." Jack got up and picked up her coat.

"Is this case getting to be too much?" Coleson said, appearing behind Jack.

"It's not too much, Coleson," Jack said, glaring at him.

"Who's this?" Coleson said, nodding at Emmaline. "Another phony psychic consultant charging the force ninety dollars an hour?"

Emmaline made an indignant noise and narrowed her eyes like she was going to say something. Jack jumped in.

"You got nothing better to do, Coleson? Sergeant not trusting you with any cases anymore? Butt out of my job, and don't address my special consultant," Jack said, through gritted teeth.

"Touchy, touchy," Coleson said. He raised his hands palm up like he thought Jack was about to attack him. "Don't get your panties in a twist."

"The very fact you mentioned my panties is fucking inappropriate," Jack said. She turned to point at him, stabbing her finger towards his chest but not touching him. "Leave us alone. We're solving a case. Go update your Instagram or whatever it is people like you do."

"Was that a burn?" Coleson asked, laughing. He had backed to the wall, as if her poking finger was a loaded gun. He folded his arms and lounged against the wall, smirking, although Piper thought he might be rattled. "Because I don't think it landed."

"Grow up, will you?" Jack said.

Emmaline stood up and pulled her coat on as Piper gathered up the papers and packed up their laptop.

"Let's go," Jack growled. She shoved her things under her arm and stalked out. Piper traded a look with Emmaline as they hurried to follow her.

Jack certainly wasn't messing around.

36

"It's down here," Piper said. They led the way to Aeva's house and knocked on the door. Emmaline felt nervous, she sort of hated confrontation, and although she was generally able to handle it when it came up, coming to someone's house and demanding answers was uncomfortable.

She rubbed the beads of her prayer bracelet between her fingers and wished she'd rescued more of her things from the house before fleeing it. Maybe Raphael would hook her up with some more charms and foci.

"Em, do you need to, like, do anything special to find out what kind of mage she is?" Jack asked. She raised her eyebrow at Emmaline who snapped back to reality.

"Ah, no. I'll hang back and see what I can see. There are no marks on the door that I can sense, so I guess she's not a big target to the hunters..."

The door opened and Aeva answered, she was in pyjamas and a black silk robe. Her hair was in disarray, and there were dark bags under her eyes. "Hello?"

"Jack Duarte, I'm with the police," Jack said. She flashed her badge and Aeva's eyes narrowed. "I believe you know my partner, Piper. We have a few questions for you."

"What sort of questions?" Aeva asked. She pulled the door half closed and peered out at them from the gap.

"About the disappearance of Edith Armstrong. I understand you know more than you let on to Piper the other day." Jack moved closer to the door.

"Do you have a warrant? I don't have to tell you anything unless I'm under arrest," Aeva said.

Jamie Sands

The nervousness had all turned into adrenaline, and Emmaline felt impatient. She pushed forward past Jack and Piper and placed her palm on the wood of the door. She felt the wood heat up and a little smoke escaped from under her hand. She heard Jack inhale sharply, but she fixed her eyes on Aeva.

"My name is Emmaline, I've been training in necromancy since I was fourteen years old. Let us in, or I'll send the spirits of all the chickens you've ever eaten to haunt you."

Aeva sucked her breath in before opening the door and moving back into the house. "All right, no need to make threats."

Emmaline followed her in and glanced over her shoulder to beckon Jack and Piper. "I imagine you can't use fairy testimony to get approval for a warrant?"

"Not so much. Thanks, Em," Jack said. She flashed Emmaline a smile, which warmed Em's chest instantly. She quickly looked away so as not to make it weird.

The inside of Aeva's house was half Gothic and half Wiccan. Gargoyles lined the shelves, as well as wrought-iron candelabra, bunches of dried herbs, and velvet paintings of busty women and wolves with glowing eyes. On the table in the corner of the living room, a piece of fabric was spread out with crystals and candles arranged on it to form an altar.

Aeva stood with her arms crossed, scowling at Emmaline. Emmaline looked around the house and smiled. "If you're co-operative to the investigation, Jack won't press to have you imprisoned for obstruction of justice."

Jack raised her eyebrows and moved closer to Aeva. "We have it on good authority that you paid the Wild Hunt to kidnap Edith Armstrong. Have you got anything to say about that?"

Aeva's eyes widened and she wavered, looking between the three of them. "I don't... I don't know what you're talking about."

"You do. Timaris gave us your name. I understand that under agreement, the fey don't lie." Jack folded her arms and stared daggers at the taller woman.

Aeva sat down on the edge of the sofa. "I, oh, goddess." Her voice choked off and she put her head in her hands and started to cry, her voice catching and hitching as she sobbed. "I'm so sorry. I didn't... I didn't realise what would happen. I thought it'd be a bit of fun."

"A bit of fun?" Jack asked, her voice raised in pitch with incredulity. She pulled out her phone and started recording audio. "I'm going to record this conversation. It won't be admissible in court, it's just for my own notes."

Piper went to sit beside Aeva. "How about you tell us what happened? In your own words." They gave Aeva a reassuring smile.

"I went to…" she stopped, shook herself a little, and restarted with a deep breath. "I read about the fey. I'm – I'm not a very powerful mage, but I'd heard they could teach." She looked up at Emmaline, who shrugged one shoulder, not willing to give anything away. "But, I thought I'd ask for a favour first, to get to know how they worked and – and Edith was such a grumpy old bat to me. Really, she was awful. She spat in the street when she saw me, once." Aeva frowned at her hands and wound them together.

"That sounds awful," Piper said, sympathetically. Emmaline glanced at Jack who wore the hint of a proud smile. "So, you got in touch with the fey and summoned the Wild Hunt?"

Aeva nodded and hiccupped once.

"Who told you about them?" Emmaline asked.

Aeva looked at her, wiping her streaming eyes. Her mouth worked for a moment before she spoke. "Another mage. At the magic store."

"Do you know who it was? Like, did you get a name off them?"

Aeva shook her head, one hand moving to her throat and dropping down again. She reached for a tissue and rubbed her eyes.

"You summoned them, and then what?" Jack prompted.

"I wanted them to give her a fright. To scare her off and to–" Aeva closed her eyes and forced the next words out through gritted teeth. "I know it's a shitty thing to do and I know you probably think I'm a scumbag. You'd be right. I'm a foolish scumbag. I had no idea what they'd be like, how they'd... how they'd twist things. I didn't think. I didn't have enough power to scare them, so they took her, and they took more than their pay, too."

"What did you bargain with?" Piper asked.

Aeva sucked in her breath. "I thought I was bargaining with something I didn't need. But actually, it was. I feel the lack of it – the knowledge I don't know it anymore. I thought I was giving them one memory, but they took all the memories of my grandmother. I know I had one, I have a couple pictures, but when I look at them, it's nothing. Like looking at a stranger. I don't even remember her name," Aeva sobbed. She hid her face in her hands and bent forward, crying hard.

Piper patted her shoulder. "There, there." They looked up at Emmaline, their eyes wide with concern. "Em, did they take her memories of her grandmother for good?"

Emmaline shrugged. "We have to assume so. The fairies love a bit of poetic justice. Aeva wanted a grandmother stolen, so they took what you remembered of your own grandmother. I'm sorry, Aeva, that's pretty horrible."

Jack frowned, tapping her finger on her arm. After a moment's silence, she spoke up again. "You don't know where Edith is? Timaris said they handed her to you, in Faerie."

Aeva looked up and swallowed. "I don't think so? I've not been there before, but there are some blanks in my memory since the deal was made. Maybe I was there and they took that memory, too?" She hiccupped and scrubbed at her face with the palm of her hand. "I don't know where she is. I'm so sorry."

"I think we'd better get you down to the station," Jack said. "Aeva, go get changed into something less," – she stopped, looking at Aeva and obviously struggling to come up with the appropriate words – "bedwearish. Piper, keep an eye on her."

Piper and Aeva got up and left the room, Aeva still crying and Piper trying to say soothing things.

Jack looked at Emmaline and gave her a half smile. "Thanks for your help back there, we really shouldn't have entered without her permission, or a warrant, but... well, getting information, it's a lot easier with your help."

"Of course," Emmaline smiled back, affection making it wider. "It's what I'm here for."

Jamie Sands

There was silence for a few seconds before Jack cleared her throat. "Could you really have called up the spirits of all the chickens she's ever eaten?"

Emmaline laughed. "No, of course not!" Jack's face broke into a relieved smile, so Emmaline decided to tease her. "Just the last one or two."

Jack's cheeks paled.

37

Jack frowned all through the booking and taking a statement process, which didn't particularly surprise Piper. Frowning was Jack's default expression.

"None of this is going to fly in court, though, is it?" Emmaline asked Jack, seeming to cut to the heart of it all. "All this fairy magic stuff."

"No, it wouldn't be remotely permissible. We can at least ask her to sign a statement saying she paid a gang to scare the old lady and they took it too far. We can work with that, and it's not untrue." Jack sounded a little unconvinced, though, and she was quiet as they finished off the processing.

Once Aeva was in a holding cell and Piper had signed the last piece of paperwork, they tracked down Jack, brooding in the break room.

Jamie Sands

"What's going on?" Piper asked.

"This doesn't solve the case," Jack said. "We still haven't found Edith, or the reverend. Why would the Wild Hunt take Aeva's bargain and then mess with her, stealing her memories? Why doesn't she remember being in Faerie?"

"Maybe because they're fey and they're unpredictable?" Emmaline suggested. Piper looked over to see her lounging in the corner of the room, her fingers playing with the knotted string on her wrist.

Jack glanced around the room. They weren't alone. There were a few officers eating their lunch who had fallen suspiciously silent, eavesdropping.

"We can't have this conversation here, we need to get moving," Jack picked up her jacket and tossed the car keys to Piper. "You're driving, I need to think."

"Where are we going?" Piper asked, catching the keys and following. Emmaline hopped up to follow as well.

"I think it's time to stop putting off talking to Abel Armstrong."

The drive to the library was uncharacteristically quiet as Jack stared out the window and occasionally muttered to herself. As they got onto the motorway, Jack turned to look at Emmaline in the back seat.

"While we were talking to Aeva, did you notice anything, um, sense anything magically?"

Emmaline chewed on her lower lip then shook her head. "There was no active magic being done, if that's what you mean."

"I noticed a few times it seemed like she was going to say something and said something else. Could that have been a fey thing?" Jack asked.

"Maybe," Emmaline shrugged. "I'm sure they have ways of binding the tongue. Actually, I know a spell which does a similar thing, it's common. If I had done some prep before we talked to her I could probably have seen if a spell was working." Emmaline paused and tugged on the string on her wrist. "Actually, I probably still could, if you want to ask her more in the station."

"Are you saying the magic might have been there, but not active?"

"It's hard to explain," Emmaline said. "The spell would have been set previously, like, whenever the thing happened, say, when the fey put the *geas* on her."

"*Geas?*" Piper asked.

"It's like a compulsion, or a binding. But the effect is ongoing, so like, it's not a flare of magic, so much as a low-level buzz.

Like *musak* playing in the supermarket as opposed to a live band."

Jack nodded and turned back to the window, staring out of it.

"I'm not sure I followed any of that," Piper said.

"Sorry, it's hard to explain in a way which makes sense if you don't know magic," Emmaline said. "A *geas* is like a compelling thing, like if I put a *geas* on you it might mean you could only tell the truth, or you could never speak my name."

Piper nodded. "Okay, so the *musak* thing?"

"Um, how about instead of *musak* you think of it like when you put on the TV channel which is all music videos. So, you first turn on the TV, then you get the loudness, like, 'whoa, the TV's on and it's playing music' and it takes all your attention, right?" Emmaline leaned forward, warming to the subject.

"Sure," Piper said.

"And once it's been on for a while you can mostly ignore it, but it's definitely still there. Background magic is like that. So much of the world has its own magic. Places have residues, mages have an aura. You kind of have to tune it out on some level."

"Got it," Piper said, and smiled at Emmaline in the rear view mirror. "Thanks for simplifying it for me."

"Any time. I guess I'm not that used to explaining it to non-mages. It's a good exercise for me, too," Emmaline said. "When you grow up with this stuff it's kinda normal and you don't have to have it laid out."

"'Normal' for me growing up was a roast for lunch on Sundays," Piper said. They both looked at Jack expectantly.

"My father raised me in the army," Jack said. "Normal was mess halls and rides in the green trucks."

The Other Side of the Mirror

"That explains so much," Emmaline said, shaking her head.

38

The library Abel worked in was a medium-sized suburban library attached to a community centre. Libraries like this always felt familiar to Jack. Everywhere she'd lived as a kid, she'd always found a local library. It was a good place to sit and be around people without it costing money, plus there were always books about mysteries...

There were two people behind the counter wearing lanyards with IDs attached, a few people sitting and reading, one examining the newspaper with a magnifying glass, and a tall white man with rounded shoulders pushing a trolley full of books around the shelves.

"He looks like our guy," Jack said to Piper and Emmaline. She made a beeline for him.

He wore a plain grey button-down shirt and dark jeans. He had earbuds in, attached to a dated iPhone. He looked up as they approached and shelved a book before pulling out his earbuds. "Can I help you?"

"Abel Armstrong?" Jack asked, showing him her badge. "I'm Detective Jack Duarte, we'd like to ask you a couple of questions. Is there a private place we can talk?"

Abel didn't look spooked, or even particularly surprised. He looked more tired than anything. He nodded and moved the trolley of books to the end of the aisle, parking it against the end of the bookshelf.

"I guess we can use the staff break room?" Abel said. "It's this way." He led them back behind the counter, giving a quick explanation to the librarians stationed there. They looked at Jack and Piper's badges and one of them signed the three of them into a guestbook.

Jamie Sands

The staff-room was a clean, somewhat bare room with a table, several chairs, and a battered couch. There was a modest kitchenette with tea and coffee-making supplies and a microwave. Not unlike some of the rooms at the police station, really.

"How can I help you, Detective?" Abel asked, sitting at the table. Piper sat opposite Abel, and Jack sat beside them. Emmaline took the couch, folding her arms to watch.

"Do you mind if we record this?" Jack asked, pulling out her phone.

"What is this about?"

"I'm assuming you're aware that your mother Edith is missing?" Jack asked. "An officer called for your alibi."

"Am I under arrest?" Abel asked. "Is the recording going to be used in court?"

"No, you're not under arrest. Your alibi is solid. We just need some more information you might be able to provide."

"Okay, sure, I don't mind you recording it." Abel folded his hands on the table.

Jack tapped her phone, checked it was recording, then met Abel's eyes. "When was the last time you saw your mother?" Jack asked.

"Let me think," Abel looked out the window for a moment. "I guess the last time I spoke to her was during the trial. I tried to visit her after I was acquitted, but she had a friend over who turned me away. I didn't try to visit again after that. She's never been in touch."

"At the trial, so this was, what? Over twenty years ago?" Jack asked.

"Bit longer. I was in for ten years before the acquittal and I've been here since, started in the community outreach programme," Abel said. He smiled slightly, then looked serious again.

"Right, and you were initially convicted of killing your sister Myrtle's lover, correct?"

"That's right. At the time I was involved with some bad people. Some people with simplistic views about the world." Abel's mouth twisted bitterly as he spoke. "Myrtle was dating this guy, Eddy, and he wasn't right for her. That's what I believed, at the time." Abel sighed, looking out the window for a moment, the corners of his mouth pulling down.

"Not right in what way?" Jack asked.

"He just wasn't. These people were adamant about it. They were a gang, a kind of 'religious purity' thing. I don't know if they're still around, but they were pretty intense."

"Hey, do you need some water?" Piper asked, getting up to fetch it for him when he nodded.

"It's warm in here. I'm sorry, talking about back then makes me sorta anxious, I'm sure you get why." Abel rubbed his forehead with the sleeve of his shirt. It came away slightly damp.

"I understand, really," Jack said. "Take your time. What was the name of the group you were involved in? Was it a church thing, or?"

"They didn't really have a name, although it was pretty well organised," Abel took a ragged breath and rolled up his sleeves, nodding and thanking Piper as they placed a cup of water down in front of him.

Jack saw something on the inside of his wrist – something familiar which sent a chill down her spine.

"Is that...?" She leaned forward, took hold of his forearm, and turned it slightly so the light hit the symbol branded into his skin. "Em, this is the same mark Amy has, right?"

Jamie Sands

Em crossed the room and peered at Abel's arm. Then she looked into his face.

"You were a mage hunter?"

Abel flinched, but quickly schooled his face. "I don't know what that means."

"We know about mages and hunters, and a fair few things besides," Jack said. "I get assigned to unusual cases, so you don't need to pretend you don't know what we're talking about. And we'd really rather you were straight up about whatever you know."

Abel's eyes flicked to the recording phone. Jack caught the look. "No one outside this room will hear the recording. You can speak freely about whatever you need to."

Abel was silent for a long minute, looking Jack in the eye and breathing slowly and deeply. She returned his gaze, because it felt like what he needed her to do.

Finally, he turned his arm so the mark was to the table top, shook his head and turned it mark-up again.

"I'm ashamed of it. I almost cut this out of my arm one night in prison, but my cellmate saw me with the blade and panicked, called in the guards." He went silent for a moment, remembering, and seemed to shake himself out of it. "How do you know about the hunters?"

"I'm a mage, and hunters attacked me the other night," Emmaline said. She sat in Piper's seat. Jack felt a kind of repressed, buzzing anger from her and hoped she could keep it inside.

"This guy you killed, Eddy, he was a mage?" Jack asked. This was the clue she'd been missing, she could feel it in her gut, but how it all connected wasn't quite clear yet.

"That's right. My mother, Edith, she was in the order, too, or she'd used to be," Abel said. "She got me into it."

Jamie Sands

"Wait – Edith was in the Order of Mage Hunters as well?"

Jack and Piper exchanged looks of surprise.

"Right. She was mostly in an advisory role when she got me involved. She left Myrtle out of it, Myrtle was always fragile. You know? Anxious and sickly." Abel's face contorted with pain.

"And from what you know, what happened to Myrtle?" Emmaline asked.

"She took her own life pretty soon after the trial." Abel hung his head. "Lord, if I could take it all back, you know I would. I did my time, I healed. I reformed. I saw the order had put so much hate into my heart and then abandoned me. They're nothing. They were like the KKK, or something. Ignorant and afraid and violent for no good reason. I got no reason to hate people, just because they can do something I can't." He dabbed at his eyes and took a drink of water.

"I'm sorry about your sister," Piper said. They sat down beside him and put their hand on his shoulder. He brought his hand up to rest on theirs and nodded.

"Thank you."

"So, let me get this totally straight. Myrtle's boyfriend was a mage?" Emmaline asked.

"Yeah. My mum, Edith, she said he had put a spell on Myrtle. She said Myrtle wasn't aware of what she was doing with him – like he was some kind of evil wizard from a fairy tale twisting her will to his," Abel said.

He took another slow breath, gathering himself before continuing. "It sounded far-fetched, but my mother never lied to me, I had no reason to doubt her. The mage hunters... they could do some weird stuff, too, unexplainable. Maybe they did something to me as well."

"If you killed Eddy, then why would this business be flaring up again now, do you think?" Jack asked, carefully. She didn't want to sound blunt when he was clearly suffering.

"How is it flaring up again? You think they were part of the reason Mum disappeared?" Abel laid his palms gently on the table and looked at her, his eyebrows drawn together.

"Edith went missing out of the house. Mysterious circumstances. It looks like mages and fey are involved. They left a note which said *A debt is paid*, do you know what it might be in reference to?" Jack asked.

Abel was silent for a moment before looking up and meeting Jack's eyes. "I mean, maybe it's an eye for an eye thing. I took one of theirs, so they're taking one of ours?"

"But you're not in the order anymore," Emmaline said. "And the timing is weird. Why get revenge this many years later? They could've done it right away, way back then."

"Do you know anything about the church your mother goes to? The reverend from there went missing last night," Jack asked.

"She's still going to that one near her house? They're..." Abel trailed off, gathering his thoughts. "The church has nothing to do with the order, they're good folks. Unless she's moved and is at a new church, but mum always said she'd never move once she put down roots."

"Our records said she's lived in the same place for more than forty years," Piper said.

"Yeah, from what I know of that place they're, like, the opposite of the order," Abel said.

"She must've been employing some serious doublethink to be at an inclusive church on one hand and in the order on the other. But I guess she wouldn't be the first person in the world to be a hypocrite," Jack said. "Was she a member of both at the same time?"

Abel shook his head. "When it was the order, it was all the order. I guess the reality of things hit her, and she gave it up. She didn't go to church while she was involved in the order."

"Well, maybe that makes sense," Emmaline said. "From what Amy's told me, the order demands a lot of time, even from its normal human members, not just the trained assassins like she was."

"Abel, this has all been really helpful. But I need to know if you remember Eddy having any friends, any mage buddies who might've been out for revenge, or something like that?" Jack wasn't sure he'd put up with too many more questions, the conversation was having a toll on him and she didn't want to push it.

Abel thought for a moment. "Yeah, there were a couple. Um, a guy called Deacon, maybe a woman was arrested, too. Or maybe the order took her out. It's sorta hard to remember. I never took the training or studied their lists of mages, but I do remember when they told me about Eddy there were a couple others close to him."

"Deacon," Emmaline hissed.

"Do you know Deacon's last name?" Jack asked.

Abel shook his head. "Only thing I can remember about him was that I thought it must've been a name he gave himself, because he looked like a Japanese dude, and I've never heard of a Japanese dude called Deacon."

"Sounds like the same Deacon to me," Piper said.

Jack handed Abel her card and tried to give him a reassuring smile. "Thanks, Abel. This has been really helpful. Listen, I know you're out of touch with your mother but anything you can remember from that time might be helpful. You let us know if you come up with anything else, all right?"

"Of course," Abel took the card and gave them all a watery smile. "I hope you find her."

As they walked out of the library, Jack's heart pinged a little. His mother had set him up for a horrible act and disowned him when he did it. And yet, he still hoped that they would find her.

Families...

39

"That was a wild ride," Piper said, buckling their seat belt. They were in the back seat now, Jack behind the steering wheel, and their mind was spinning after the conversation they'd just had with Abel.

"I can't believe Edith was in the order," Emmaline said. She wrinkled her nose up.

"I just need to clarify. I mean, this is the same order. The same murderers who appeared out of nowhere last night and attacked you in your house?" Jack asked.

"I can't believe you were attacked," Piper said, frowning. It made their heart race a little to think of people coming after sweet, gentle Emmaline. "I hate that."

Jamie Sands

Emmaline turned to Piper and patted their arm. "It's okay, I'm okay. I got out in time, and they didn't follow me, I'm sure of it."

Piper tried to be comforted, but their mind raced. They made a mental numbered list to try and sort out their thoughts.

One: how did an organisation like that survive in New Zealand? Surely there couldn't be that many mages around to sustain an organisation of mage hunters. It wasn't like mages were having pride parades or anything.

Two: how'd they track Emmaline down when she'd only been in the country a couple of weeks, and Aeva had apparently lived in the same place for ages, unnoticed? They couldn't be that effective of a secret society.

"How'd you get away from them, Emmaline?" They asked, finally.

"They always seem to forget we can do magic," Emmaline said. "I mean, I'm quick to react, and I'm always half expecting something bad to happen, anyway."

"How did they find you, do you think?" Jack asked, seeming to echo Piper's thoughts. "It seems weird that you've been here a while with nothing, and then we see your brother who is with an ex-mage hunter and suddenly, they find you."

"Raphael would never tell them where I am!" Emmaline exclaimed, indignant.

"I wasn't saying that," Jack said quickly. "I just wondered if they were tracking him somehow and they found you because he went back into the mirror. But I don't know if that's a thing they can do."

"Urgh, you're probably right. Sod them," Emmaline said.

"So rough," Piper said. "No, but like, what'd you do to get away? Did you teleport through a mirror?"

"No, I distracted them, used a spirit to cause a ruckus," Emmaline said. "Then I ran outside in my pyjamas. Wasn't my best night, but you don't have to worry about me."

There was a silence as Jack pulled onto the southwestern motorway. The southwestern took them past a mix of houses and big old trees. It put Piper in mind of the suburbs back home in Christchurch – the same amount of green and old-school houses.

"We're going to talk to Deacon again, right?"

"Right," Jack said. "This feels like the missing link we needed to crack the case open."

Emmaline giggled. "Did you really just say that?"

"Yes, I did?" Jack side eyed Emmaline. "Why?"

"It sounded exactly like what someone in a cop movie would say. Like, an overwritten cop movie." She giggled again and

Piper grinned, too, although they were nervous of Jack getting angry.

"Maybe they'd write them like that because it's accurate?" Jack clicked her tongue playfully at Emmaline.

"You're in a good mood all of a sudden," Emmaline said.

"Because we're close to cracking the case," Piper guessed.

"I feel like we're close enough to smell the solution, the unravelling of the whole, messy conspiracy," Jack said, she slapped the steering wheel with the palm of her hand. "It feels good."

Jack drove quickly, and they arrived at Deacon's house in no time.

"Now, last time we were here, Deacon did something with his eyes." Jack turned to face Emmaline. "What was it, and how do we avoid it?"

"Mind magic," Emmaline said. "He's a bit on the... well. Mind manipulation, black magic side of things. He said your will was strong, so I think you're safe from it, more or less."

"Piper, though?" Jack glanced back. Piper felt obvious and young, their will wasn't as strong as Jack's, it couldn't be, or Deacon would've said something.

Their stomach sank as they realised they were a liability.

And what's more, they'd panicked last time they'd talked to Deacon. What if that happened again?

"I can tell when he's doing it, so I can intervene. It's much harder to resist if you don't know what's happening," Emmaline said, and blinked her wide blue eyes at Jack.

"Double negatives," Piper said. "It's tricky."

"If you're aware, it's harder for him to do," Emmaline said. "Imagine a wall inside your head and try and focus on that. Just keep thinking of the wall. It should help."

"Got it. Build a wall inside my head," Piper said. "Like meditation and visualisation."

"Exactly. You do a lot of meditation?" Emmaline sounded pleased. "That'll help."

"I have an app on my phone, it's really good," Piper said. "Although I sometimes fall asleep during them."

Jack's phone buzzed with a text message. She glanced at the screen, frowned, and dismissed the notification.

"Let's shake this guy down," Jack said.

"Just like in a noir movie," Emmaline said, giggling.

"I did that one on purpose," Jack said, with a smile. "For the amusement of both of you."

40

Emmaline knocked on Deacon's door in precisely the same place she'd knocked the last time. Jack squinted at the door, trying to see what she was avoiding.

"Are the wards invisible?"

Emmaline nodded. "Yes. But I can also feel where they are, sense them." She knocked again and raised her voice. "Deacon!? Are you home?"

The door opened and a man they didn't recognise opened the door. He had mousey-brown hair, and sunken eyes. His voice was hushed, strained. "Can I help you?"

"We're looking for Deacon," Jack said. "Is he in?"

"Deacon? He's asleep. Are you here for a, y'know, business thing?" The man looked around them, then both ways up and down the street. He winked at Jack and clicked his tongue.

"I'm Detective Duarte, I'm here on police business." Jack gave him her full no-nonsense, hard-boiled detective face.

"Oh." The man stepped back and opened the door for them. "Better come in. I'll go wake him up. Mind your step."

"What's your name?" Jack asked, but the man was already trotting down the hall and up a set of stairs. Jack, Emmaline, and Piper entered the house. Emmaline shivered as she had last time and made a *hmm* noise.

"*Hmm?*" Piper asked, looking at her.

"The wards. They're different. Like, another mage has added some with different magic. It feels not like Deacon," Emmaline said.

Jamie Sands

"Another mage. Was that man a mage?" Jack asked. She stopped at a shelf of books and scanned the spines. The first few shelves were mundane stuff– classic novels and gardening manuals. Then she found volumes on psychology, phrenology, and the teachings of Aleister Crowley, and it started feeling a little more esoteric.

"I think so. He had a tattoo on his hand which could be for wind magic," Emmaline said. "Looks sorta like one my brother has."

They heard thumps and a door slamming upstairs. After a moment, the man came back downstairs again. "He's up now, he'll be down in a moment. Take a seat." He led them into the living area. He ticked his tongue against his teeth as he walked. The sound put Jack's nerves on edge.

They followed him through and sat in the tatty chairs. Piper removed a particularly alarming pillow with a surprised-looking needlepoint cat on it.

Deacon appeared a few moments later, sleep rumpled in a grey T-shirt with a slim, sexy girl anime character on it, track pants, and his hair standing on end.

"Hey, it's you lot again. What's up this time?" Deacon said. He rubbed his hand through his hair, making it stand up even more.

"Good morning to you, too," Emmaline said.

"The case we're working at the moment, it's a missing persons case, and we have reason to believe there's magic and the fey involved in how this woman disappeared," Jack said. "We think you can help out with that."

"You do, do you? I thought you already had a mage," he said. He looked pointedly at Emmaline.

"I'm not local," she said. "We need local."

"We need a local expert and you're familiar with the fey elements, especially Melchizedek," Jack said. "If there's weirdness around, I'm sure you're aware of it. And we can compensate you, if that's what you're concerned about."

Jack watched Deacon's eyes narrow and he pursed his lips as he gazed back at her.

"Hey, Eddy, would you make me a coffee?" Deacon asked, turning to the other man. "She's using big words and I'm still asleep."

"Eddy...?" Piper breathed.

"Our Eddy is dead," Jack said, shaking her head. "It's a common name."

Eddy looked between them and his eyes widened. "I gotta step out for a moment," he said. "I'll go get coffee, that'd be..." He coughed. "Yes, that'd be fine. Coffee, like the man said. See ya!" He turned to leave the apartment.

"Wait!" Emmaline said, leaping to her feet. "You do have a—" She broke off, her head making little circles as she looked all around him. *As if reading an aura,* Jack thought. "Eddy, are you resurrected? You are, aren't you?"

Eddy froze, then made a weird gesture with his hand. A blast of cold air swept through the house, buffeting Emmaline back into her seat.

Deacon ducked behind the couch. "What's going on?" He cried out.

Emmaline stood again. Her expression was thunderous. She started chanting in a language Jack didn't recognise. Digging in the pocket of her borrowed pants, she pulled out a handful of white powder, which was probably salt, and threw it towards Eddy. As Jack watched, she saw a shape coalescing into a long-limbed humanoid figure made of mist. It grabbed at Eddy's arms.

Jack started to stand and felt a hand on her shoulder, holding her down.

41

Piper was having trouble breathing deeply. Things had happened so fast. Eddy tried to duck away from the weird spectre, but the spirit chased him.

Deacon, from his hiding place behind Jack, reached a hand forward and grabbed her shoulder. Piper could see him murmuring urgently into her ear.

Jack's face was pale, and her teeth were firmly clenched together, her eyes wide and furious.

Piper reached for their baton and slowly drew it, moving so as not to gain anyone's attention yet.

Eddy grasped a medallion that hung around his neck and whipped his head towards Emmaline, crying out a word which stung Piper's ears to hear it.

Jamie Sands

Vines started to coil and push through the floorboards below Emmaline's feet, twisting around her ankles. She made a frustrated noise and leapt backwards, shoulder rolling as she crouched, and got back to her feet near Piper.

Jack's hand was on her pepper spray, but she wasn't doing anything with it. Deacon continued to speak in her ear and Piper could see his fingers digging into Jack's shoulder.

Jack needed help. This was Piper's big moment to be a hero, they just had to swallow their panic and do the thing. They could do this.

Emmaline's hand moved, catching Piper's eyes. Digging in her pocket again, she started to sing. It was a melodic song in what Piper thought was possibly Thai because she didn't recognise any Mandarin or Japanese words. She threw another handful of salt towards Eddy and this time a solid form coalesced over the spectre, making the previous ghostly thing look real, a monster made of flesh and bone.

Piper shuddered as the nightmare grabbed at Eddy's throat, their heart sped faster and faster as Eddy thrashed away, falling against the bookshelf. He gestured, and there was a cracking noise as more vines pushed up through the floorboards, splintering them. They were going for Emmaline.

"Stop it right there, Eddy!" Piper gripped their baton.

The vines continued to grow as Eddy ducked around the slow-moving beast Emmaline had summoned.

Jack made a strangled noise of frustration, her fingers flexing on the handle of her taser. But she seemed unable to do more.

Emmaline continued to sing, raising her arms up over her head and looking intensely at her shadow beast. Her eyes seemed to have a silver sheen to them.

"Fuck," Piper muttered. They swung the baton and connected solidly with Eddy's knee. Eddy cried out and fell, curling into his side on the floor. His other leg kicked Deacon's ankle, setting him off balance.

The vines wilted uselessly into the cracked floorboards.

Jack turned, shouted an angry noise, and punched Deacon in the face. She stood and aimed her pepper spray at his face.

"You want some of this?"

"No." He raised his hands up in surrender.

Emmaline breathed a sigh of relief and lowered her arms. The shadow beast stilled, seeming to look at her, waiting for the next command.

Eddy lay on the ground, curled on his side and whimpering. Deacon staggered onto the couch, holding his face.

"I can't believe I actually hit him," Piper said. Their hands shook a little and they wiped their free palm on their thigh. "I mean, you train for these things but it's different in the moment."

"You did great," Jack said. She crossed the room and squeezed Piper's arm. Piper smiled at her, grateful.

"Thanks, Jack."

"I need to get one thing straight," Jack said, turning to Deacon and then to Emmaline. "Abel went to prison for killing Eddy. But this is Eddy, right? Standing here? Alive?"

"Uh-huh," Emmaline said.

"And now he's walking and talking," Jack said. "I didn't just dream that?"

"Yes, he is," Deacon said.

"How is this possible?" Piper breathed.

Jamie Sands

"Resurrection is a thing we can do. But it's risky, very risky. It's pretty frowned upon in the white magic circles," Emmaline said. She twisted her hand and the shadow beast swirled in the air and rushed, mist like, into her pocket.

"Which would be a problem if I was a white mage," Deacon said, slowly. His voice was rougher now, and he dropped his hand to his lap to frown at them. "I'm not. I'm unseelie fey trained, and I don't care about playing nicey-nice. My best friend was killed by those monsters and I did what I had to do to bring him back."

Eddy sat up, shakily, groaning as he put some of his weight on his injured leg. Emmaline had one hand on his shoulder, and she directed him into the armchair, which he collapsed into gratefully.

"Risky how?" Piper asked.

"With resurrection, you're playing with the big forces. Even if you're a highly trained necromancer then it's kinda fifty-fifty on whether you're bringing someone back or plunging into death yourself. And on top of that, there's the risk that what you bring back isn't that person. Basically, it's dangerous," Emmaline said. Her expression was steel, utterly confident in herself and angry at the men.

"I came back just fine," Eddy said. But he didn't meet anyone's eyes.

"You came back fine, it was the time in Faerie that…" Deacon trailed off.

"Well, there are no laws against resurrection on account of it being fucking impossible," Jack said, as if trying to puzzle something out.

"There are laws against kidnapping, though. Right, Jack?" Piper asked, grinning and holding their baton at their side, ready to strike again if the need arose.

"Right. Where's Edith? And why the hell was there a twenty-year delay before you did anything?" Jack stepped closer to the couch and loomed over Deacon.

"I, uh, well. I don't do necromancy. I had to make a bargain with the fey, and the bargain I made..." He swallowed, his throat working and a dry croak coming out before he shook his head. "I don't think I can talk about it. But that's why."

"Why can't you talk about it?" Jack asked.

"Words bound," Deacon said, he gestured at his own throat. "Y'know, magically."

"A geas!" Piper interjected. Deacon gave them a surprised look and nodded.

"After the ritual, after I woke again, I had to live in Faerie," Eddy said, frowning. "Serving the fey, trapped there with them while Myrtle..." He looked down and shook his head, drew a heavy breath. His shoulders were tense, pulled up under his ears. "While my true love killed herself mourning me. Imagine if she'd known I was alive over there, we could have... She would have waited." He stopped and took a deep, rattling breath. "But I couldn't – the fey wouldn't let me. Once I was back in this world, we had to plan. There were so many contingencies. I wanted the best possible revenge. There were so many years, so many more than twenty over there, waiting. Thinking. Imagining how I could strangle her with my own hands." His hands tensed into fists briefly. "But I thought up something even better with Deac."

"I don't need to hear you congratulate yourselves on your plan. Tell us where Edith is so we can bring her and the reverend back," Jack said, her voice hard. It threatened worse than pepper spray if they didn't comply.

Deacon and Eddy exchanged glances before Deacon replied.

"We don't know where the reverend is. But Edith's in a pocket dimension I set up."

"Is a pocket dimension a thing you can get her back from?" Jack asked, running a hand through her hair. "Like, now?"

"And what happened to the reverend, then?" Piper asked.

Deacon shrugged. "He knew about the fey, and he suspected something—"

"We may have talked to the Wild Hunt about making him vanish," Eddy finished.

"Can you get them back?" Jack asked. It sounded like she was barely keeping a reign on her anger.

"We can get Edith back," Deacon said.

"But why should we?" Eddy cut in.

"Kidnapping is a crime," Jack said. She took hold of Deacon's collar and yanked on it. "And if you don't retrieve that woman, Emmaline will set one of her ghosty things to haunt you forever. And I'll go through all your records and find every single time you've skimped on taxes, run a red light, jaywalked, or pocketed a piece of food without paying for it. I'll have you in court twice a week until you die."

There was a long pause while Deacon looked up at Jack's face, aghast.

Eddy looked between Jack and Deacon, then over to Emmaline and Piper, and waved a hand. He slumped back on the couch and sighed. "To be honest, I thought revenge would feel better than this. You don't have to threaten us."

Jack looked at Eddy in surprise. "What?"

"Maybe it was the twenty – or more like forty – years stuck in Faerie, but I feel uneasy, uncertain, undone thinking of her in there, all alone. Lonely."

Deacon rolled his eyes. "Your brain is addled since your years in Faerie. You don't know what you want from one moment to the next." He sighed heavily and went to stand. "Fine. I'll have to get some tools, though."

"I'll go with you," Emmaline said, patting Eddy on the shoulder. "You can stay right where you are, Eddy."

"Are we going to be able to arrest people?" Piper asked Jack, their mind trying to piece it all together. "Eddy's legally dead, and Deacon's like the middleman for dealing with the fey."

Jack huffed her breath out and looked hard at Eddy. "I think we can work something out. Maybe Eddy faked his death to frame Abel and has been lying in wait until the perfect moment, or something like that."

"What I did wasn't on the up and up, I get that," Eddy said, his eyes wild. He leaned forward, one hand reaching for Jack until she stepped out of his reach and he let it drop again. "But you gotta see it from my point of view. She didn't tell her daughter she couldn't date me. She asked her son to kill me. Because I happen to have magic."

Jack sat down and rubbed her eyes, groaning in frustration. She rubbed her forehead and started muttering to herself.

Eddy and Piper watched her for a moment. Piper thought maybe it was best to jump in and give Jack something to go off.

"The fact is, it's ethically complicated," Piper said. "I mean, you didn't kill her, which would be, like, standard eye for an eye."

"First things first, we have to get the both of them back in this world, this side of the mirror," Jack said. "We can charge Eddy with faking his own death and kidnapping Edith. That's a good couple of decades in prison."

Emmaline and Deacon returned to the room. Deacon looked upset to have heard what Jack had just said. "No, please. I'll bring her back, then there's no need for a charge of kidnapping, yes?"

Eddy looked at Deacon in surprise. "What?"

"I'm sure there can be nothing you can accuse me of legally, except giving him a place to live," Deacon said, and for once his voice wasn't laced with amusement or irony. "Eddy has been through a lot, and his mind isn't what it was. I know I shouldn't have helped with this whole plan, but I'd rather he stay in my house, where I can keep an eye on him."

"Your co-operation will go a long way," Jack said.

"And if you don't do what she says, I'll hex the crap out of you so you can never sleep," Emmaline said, her voice sweet but deadly.

Deacon met Jack's eyes and then Emmaline's, shuddered slightly, and nodded. "Fine."

Deacon held a snow globe in one hand. It had a little castle inside it. In his other hand, he had a box of candles and a book of matches. Emmaline walked slightly behind him, and Piper caught sight of a misty shape hovering over Emmaline's shoulder. Maybe it was the same being she'd summoned earlier, but it was very hard to see much in the way of distinguishing features.

"A simple ritual," Emmaline said. Her voice was steel, warning him not to contradict.

"Yeah, simple," Deacon said.

Jamie Sands

Emmaline narrowed her eyes at him. "And if you even think about using your freaking mind-control powers on Jack again, or Piper, then you will regret it."

Jack raised her head and looked at them both. "Yeah, I hated that. No more of any of your shit."

Deacon set the globe down on his coffee table, which, now Piper looked at it, had some burn and blast marks on it. The desks in the chemistry lab at their school had looked similar, a visual history of experiments gone wrong. He arranged four candles around the globe.

"At the compass points," he said, looking up to meet Piper's eyes. "Since you seem so interested."

Eddy sat on the opposite side of the table to Deacon and sighed, wiping his head. "This was *such* a good spell," he said.

"I don't care if it was the fucking Sistine Chapel of spells," Jack said, through gritted teeth. "Fucking bring her back. Right now."

Emmaline stood over the two men with her arms folded. "Don't try any funny business or I'll tell my pet spirits to drag you into the dimension of Death."

Eddy shuddered violently, his hands gripping the edge of the seat and his eyes rolling until he got control of himself again.

"I don't want to go back there," he said, his voice unsteady.

Deacon lit the candles, speaking some indistinct words to each of them as he did it. Finally he nodded to Eddy. "It's ready. Tell me what you need."

Eddy took Deacon's hand and started to speak in a language Piper didn't recognise. Emmaline's ghostly summoning stood over her shoulder, both of them watching the two men.

Jamie Sands

Piper shuddered and wrapped their arms around themself. Their stomach was twisted, aching with stress and nervousness. They felt a hand on their shoulder and started, turning to see Jack give them a smile. They relaxed a little.

"I think it's Gaelic they're speaking," she said. "I half recognise it."

"How can you half recognise Gaelic?" Piper asked

"Dad was posted in Scotland for six months when I was eleven," Jack said. "We lived over there."

"There is so much about you I don't know," Piper murmured. Their rapidly beating heart and fear of the magic taking place a few feet away gave them courage to say what they were thinking.

If they were about to explode from a spell gone wrong, at least they would've spoken their mind. Jack's expression was surprised and then softened.

"Once all this is wrapped up, we can go get a drink together,"

Jack said. "And we'll talk."

Piper swallowed and nodded, putting their hand over Jack's

and watching as the mages started their work.

42

The magic swelled in the room as Eddy spoke the ancient spell. Emmaline could feel the air thrumming, setting her hairs on end and giving her goosebumps.

The snow globe sat on the coffee table but inside the glass dome the glitter and little plastic stars started to swirl over the plastic castle.

It must have looked eerie to Piper and Jack. Emmaline flicked her eyes up to look at them, but they seemed to be relaxed enough, talking to each other. Jack glanced over and nodded slightly before giving her attention back to Piper. Emmaline guessed she was keeping them at ease to ward off a possible panic attack.

Emmaline refocused on Eddy, putting aside the warm affection she'd felt watching Jack. The important thing was keeping the men on the spell to get Edith back. So far, they seemed to be doing what they said they would, but Emmaline knew better than to let her guard down.

The air shimmered over the coffee table and a purple portal started to coalesce in mid-air. Emmaline swallowed, dread rising in her chest. "Do we need to go in there to get her?"

Deacon caught her eye and nodded, still chanting. Emmaline sighed.

"I'm going with you. Jack, we won't be long," she said.

She looked up to ensure Jack had heard. Jack eyed the portal and then Emmaline, her face ashen. "Should I come, too?"

Deacon shook his head and finished his part of the chant. "The less the better."

"One of the men should stay here," Jack said, frowning. "So that they have to bring you back safely."

Jamie Sands

Emmaline shook her head this time. "Eddy has to come to speak the spell, and I won't leave you two with Deacon. He might try some mind magic on you and you couldn't counter it. It's safer for you this way."

Jack sighed. "Fine, but be careful."

Emmaline waited until Eddy had gone through before following. Eddy continued speaking in Gaelic. From the way the magic tugged at the air behind her, she interpreted that part of the spell kept the portal open.

Deacon stepped through behind her, and Emmaline felt uneasy. On this side of the portal, she was outnumbered. She gritted her teeth and fingered her woven bracelet, feeling the familiar tingle of the spirit she'd bound to it.

She took a deep breath of the stale air. They were in a twilight place, the light a dim and purple grey. Not quite another dimension in the same way Faerie was – or the realm of Death.

Emmaline knew the realm of Death well. She was comfortable there. This place, by contrast, was distinctly uncomfortable, like sitting on a chair that was too small.

There was a smell to it as well, more than the staleness of the air: rotting leaves and the ozone scent after a lightning strike. She looked around, seeing shapes here and there in the misty dimness.

Some looked like boxes, left on the ground or stacked in piles.

Some looked like trees, reaching long, twisted branches up out of the gloom, with things hanging off them.

"Is this your storage room?" Emmaline asked, turning to Deacon. He shrugged one shoulder then nodded, still murmuring.

Jamie Sands

"*Pas vrai*," Emmaline said. "Why've I never thought of this?"

Deacon was also looking around, moving down the path between rocks and bookshelves, set up beside each other in a semblance of order. The shelves held jars, dusty books, and weird, black-and-purple plants.

Eddy pointed to Deacon, nodding at Emmaline to follow him. Her fingers twitched, checking if she could summon spirits here. Nothing happened, no feeling of something coming the way she was used to detecting. She followed him, feeling out of her depth and hoping he couldn't tell that she was cut off from her source of power.

Down the end of the path they came to a large stone box, of the sort Emmaline was used to seeing in very expensive family tombs.

"You stored her in a casket?" Emmaline asked, aghast. She felt her stomach twist in fear for the old woman. "She's nearly eighty. Are you sure she's still alive?" Emmaline instinctively sent out her death sense to see if she could feel Edith's spirit, but she felt nothing.

"Alive, yes," Deacon said. Eddy moved to the end of the casket, clicked his fingers three times, and levered it open with one hand. Emmaline felt the frisson of the charm he'd performed but moved to look inside the casket.

Edith lay in state. The casket was lined with purple satin, including a little pillow. Her hands were folded over her chest but her eyes wide open, staring. Her eyeballs swivelled to focus on Emmaline.

"She's been awake this whole time?" Emmaline asked, revolted. "Undo the paralysis, for goddess's sake."

"Right, was just getting to that." Deacon leaned into the casket, bracing his hands on the edge of it so he could lean right in and place his face next to Edith's. He murmured a few words, too faintly for Emmaline to hear, and Edith's body relaxed. She shifted slightly for a moment, as if waking. She grabbed Deacon by the shirt collar and slapped him with her other hand.

"How dare you use your filthy, godless magic on me!" she cried, her voice hoarse from disuse, dry as the dead, but still ferocious. "How dare you bring me to this place!"

Emmaline chuckled, choosing not to intervene as Deacon struggled to break free of the older woman's grasp. Finally, she stepped forward.

"Ma'am, we're here to bring you out again, you're safe with me. Let's get you out of there to start with, then we'll get you back home," Emmaline said.

Deacon rubbed his face, pouting. Edith sat up, looked at Emmaline, and scowled. "And who are you to be messed up with these two rapscallions?"

"Rapscallions?" Emmaline quirked an eyebrow. "I'm part of the investigation to find you. I'm a magical consultant." She offered her arm to Edith, who eyed her suspiciously, but after a moment she took it and leaned on it heavily as she climbed out of the casket. Deacon came around to assist as well, taking Edith's other elbow.

"A magical consultant?" Edith asked. "And what does 'magical consultant' mean?"

"I'm being paid to help the police," Emmaline said, with a bright smile. "I have special... magical information." Sure, she could have got a reaction by saying she was a necromancer, but she wasn't entirely sure Abel was correct in his assumption that Edith had cut ties with the mage hunters.

Edith huffed and dusted off her skirt and shirt. "Never in my life have I had to put up with so much, this has been an ordeal and a half. I don't know who you are, young woman, but if you can get me home, I'll follow you."

"Come on, lead us back through so we can find the reverend and get this all sorted out," Emmaline said, nodding at Eddy. He hurried ahead.

"The reverend?" Edith paled even more, and her hand flew to her chest. Emmaline bit her lip. She probably shouldn't have mentioned that.

"It's all right, the first step is getting you back." Emmaline said. "We won't hurt you. That's all over with. Come on back to the real world."

"About time, too," Edith sniffed.

43

Jack watched the flickering lights of the portal with no small measure of discomfort. Emmaline and the other two mages had been gone for ten minutes.

Was there a time difference in this pocket dimension, like there was in Faerie?

They really had no way of knowing.

"Should we go through and check if they're all right?" Piper asked, but their voice wavered with fear.

Jack grimaced, tapping the fingers of one hand on the table. The other hand moved to rake through her hair. "I think it's safest if we stay here. We have no way of knowing if the portal even opens to the same place they went to, or if it switches around. Maybe it'd sense we're not magical and send us somewhere else entirely. We just don't know enough about it for it to be a calculated risk."

"Anyway, I'm sure she's fine," Piper said. "She summoned a freaking ghost creature just before. She escaped the mage hunters. She's badass."

"I'm sure you're right." But worry continued to gnaw at Jack's stomach, and would continue to do so until they reappeared. She got up and began to pace the room just to be doing something.

They startled when there was a sharp knock at the door. Jack and Piper eyed it and then each other. Jack shrugged and went to the door, looking through the peephole. On the other side of the door stood a young man, probably university aged. He had startlingly pale skin and a bright shock of red hair. He was shifting from foot to foot, peering at the peephole from the outside.

"Who is it?" Jack asked

"Um? It's Joe," he said. "I'm meeting with Deacon. I have what he wanted."

"Deacon's indisposed," Jack said. Her instinct was to open the door and let this kid in, but she had no idea what he was or if he had magic. Maybe he was on Deacon's side and would blast the two of them into oblivion to help his friend. "Just leave it on the deck, and I'll make sure he gets it."

"Are you fucking kidding me?" Joe bounced on his feet, almost dancing from side to side. "I can't! He said it had to be today, and it's not a thing I can set down and leave. Who the fuck are you?"

Jamie Sands

Jack glanced behind her and saw Piper in the hallway, frowning. Piper drew their taser and made sure it had a charge. Jack opened the door a crack.

"I'm Detective Duarte, this is Detective Gage. We're here investigating a crime, Deacon is bringing something back for us." Jack said. "Who are you?"

"Are you magic?" Piper added from behind.

"I..." Joe raised his hands, palms forward, as he met her eyes. For a moment, Jack thought he was going to throw a spell at them and braced her shoulder on the door to slam it shut. But her brain caught up and she saw he was trying to show her he was no threat. "I'm not a mage but I *am* magic. I don't want any trouble with the police."

Jack opened the door wider, one hand on her pepper spray, so he could see she'd use it in an instant. "So, what are you?"

"I'm Patupaiarehe. Uh, sort of like a changeling. I mean, I wasn't sort of a changeling, I *am* a changeling. I'm sort of Patupaiarehe." He licked his lips. "Can I come in before the neighbours notice?" He glanced behind him and then inside again.

"All right, but you keep those hands where we can see them, and no magic," Jack said.

Joe was very willing to comply, and he sat in the chair Piper pointed him to. "What case are you working that Deacon's doing this for?" Joe asked, pointing to the weird sparkling portal in the middle of the living room.

"A missing persons case," Piper said.

"Edith Armstrong, am I right?" He looked between them, seeing their expressions. "I am! That's what I had information about."

"You have information about Edith?" Jack asked. Everything was getting too weird. She couldn't keep up.

"Well, no, about her grandson." Joe's cheeks went red and he looked at the ground. "I've been giving Deacon information. He's been blackmailing me. If you could stop him doing that as part of your case, that'd be aces."

"Why would we believe you?" Piper asked, then frowned. "Wait – are you Daniel's boyfriend?"

"Yes, I'm the boyfriend. I could get out my phone and show you, if you like?" Joe said. "Please don't tease me."

Jack nodded. "Go on, show us."

Joe pulled out his phone and unlocked it, opened the messenger app, and showed the two of them some messages he'd traded with Daniel, including selfies of the two of them.

"Deacon approached me a few months ago. He knows what I am and knew that I was dating Daniel. He said he'd out me as a changeling to Dan and his family. And he'd tell my people where I am, and that would... well, he'd ruin everything for me unless I helped him out."

"You're not dating Daniel just because Deacon told you to?" Jack asked. It was just the kind of gross thing she could imagine Deacon doing. Joe shook his head.

"No, I was with him already. I guess I went to the wrong pub or café or something and Deacon saw me with Daniel," Joe sighed. "He got me to feed him a bunch of stuff, like, when Daniel would be going around to Edith's, and where the spare key is."

"Anything else?" Jack asked.

"I guess I-I," Joe looked away. "I've given him some selfies, of... of Daniel. He said he could track him that way. But I think

Deacon traded them with other people." Joe hung his head. "I really hate myself for all this, but I didn't have much choice."

"Track him with a selfie?" Piper asked.

Joe shrugged. "I'm not clear on what he does exactly, or what it means, but I put a protection over Danny, uh, Daniel, just to be safe. I don't think the mages can do too much to him."

"Do you have any recorded messages of Deacon blackmailing you?" Jack asked, her mind processing.

"I, yeah, he texted me a few times," Joe said. He flicked through the messages on his phone. "I have them saved, would that be enough?"

"Then we have something on him, in the real world," Piper said, standing a bit brighter. "Something that would stand up in court."

"And we could say he was threatening to out you as gay, and you were afraid for your safety," Jack said. "That way the magic thing doesn't have to come into it."

"I don't want to make any enemies, I just want him to leave me alone. Me and Dan…" Joe started, but his voice died away.

The sparkling portal in the centre of the room made a sound. They saw Deacon come through, stepping on the coffee table and onto the floor before turning back to help Edith. Emmaline came right after, also helping the old lady.

Eddy came through last. Once his feet were on the ground, he stopped chanting and clapped twice in succession. The portal folded in on itself and vanished.

"The fuck are you doing here?" Deacon asked. His face was drained of colour and he looked fearfully from Joe to Jack.

Jamie Sands

"He's closing the case for us," Jack said. She gave Deacon a wide, toothy smile that showed every one of her teeth, and reminded Piper of a shark.

44

"Edith is in a stable condition. We've got her on intravenous fluids to be on the safe side and some sedatives, so she can rest," the nurse said.

Jack had the nurse on speaker-phone so Piper and Emmaline could hear. Emmaline looked relieved and relaxed back in Jack's desk chair. The detective department was largely empty at this time on the weekend, and it felt almost like a private office. A large, cluttered private office.

"Thanks for all your help, Sefina, let me know if there're any changes or if she has any visitors," Jack said.

"Of course, Detective, was there anything else?"

"No, thank you."

Jamie Sands

As soon as Jack hung up the phone, it rang again. Marlo's name and an old picture of her came up on the screen. Her mouth wide, laughing, her eyes hidden under dark glasses.

Jack declined the call but twenty seconds later it rang again. Jack accepted it, sighing.

"Please don't call me, Marlo," she said, by way of greeting.

"Jack! You haven't been replying to my messages so I had to call. I want to talk to you, after the other night," Marlo began. It was a tone which Jack recognised instantly. She was about to start in on a big, seemingly heartfelt apology with all the charm loaded on.

"I'm gonna stop you right there," Jack said. She turned away from the prying eyes of Emmaline and Piper. "I'm not interested in seeing you again, you got that?"

There was a pause. Had she got through to her?

"Jackie, you don't mean that. I just want to catch up and clear the air," Marlo said. "I'm sure we can—"

"No. Not interested. Sorry, Marlo." She hung up and switched her phone to silent before pocketing it.

It was interesting to talk to Marlo and feel none of the tug that she'd used to feel. She could almost feel the lack of it, but as a distant memory with no nostalgia attached. She walked back over to her desk and leaned on the side of it.

"Who was that?" Emmaline asked with a carefully calculated indifference which didn't exactly sound genuine.

"No one," Jack said. "It doesn't matter. We need to work out how to contact the Wild Hunt and find Reverend Zebedee."

"Deacon said... uh, just let me check." Piper flipped through their notes. "He said Eddy realised, hanging out at the church for time he did, checking out Edith, that the rev knew about fairies. He left offerings for them."

Jamie Sands

"Offerings? I think I saw him setting out, like, milk in a bowl?" Jack asked.

"Sounds like a fey thing. Brownies," Emmaline said. "As far as I know, it's how the Irish used to keep the fey from meddling in their lives."

They had brought Eddy and Deacon into the station. They were in separate holding cells. Emmaline had placed small wards on the cell doors, although she had made it clear to Jack it wouldn't hold either of them for long if they tried to break out. However, neither man seemed like they were going to try. Both seemed subdued, and had been quite co-operative in questioning.

"So, the rev knew fey were a thing. Eddy said he panicked because of how close the reverend and Edith were, so he got in touch with the Wild Hunt and basically told them he didn't care what happened to him?" Piper said, reading over the notes they'd made during the interviews.

Emmaline leaned forward, her expression hard. "Which means we need to get on to this quick, because if the dark fey took him and were told it doesn't matter what happens to him, well, anything could have happened by now."

Jack breathed out heavily, her sense of urgency heightened. "We need to get back into Faerie," Jack said. She turned to Emmaline. "Can you contact your brother again?"

"I've been trying his number, but there's nothing. I'll have to use the mirror and call Gerard instead," Emmaline said. She pouted, looking around the room.

"There's a bathroom mirror, would that work?"

Emmaline nodded. "Yeah, any mirror at all."

"Just lock the door behind you and make sure no one else is in the stalls or anything," Jack said.

"You may as well come with me. If Gerard can open a portal, we can all head on through right away," Emmaline said. She stood up and pulled her thick blonde hair back into a ponytail, tying it with an elastic.

Piper frowned and looked up at Jack with large eyes. "Do I have to go, too?"

Jack looked at them and then shook her head. "Of course not. I'd rather one of us stays here in case anything happens with Edith, or one of the boys in lock up. You stay, keep your eyes on the phone and, uh, we'll be back as soon as we can."

"Thanks," Piper said. They breathed out and their shoulders slumped as they broke eye contact with Jack. "I'm sorry."

"Don't be," Emmaline said, giving Piper a quick one-armed hug. "It's safer over there with less civilians."

"I'm not a civilian," Piper said. They fingered their police badge.

"Oh – I meant, non-magical person," Emmaline said. "Nothing about your actual job." She gave Piper a warmer hug.

Jack and Emmaline headed for the bathroom.

"It's nice your bathrooms aren't gendered," Emmaline said, as they walked in.

"Especially since Piper started with us," Jack said. "It wasn't much of a problem. When they made the change, a couple people were concerned, but everyone's been so good and fine about it." She shrugged.

"Even that creepy smiley guy?" Emmaline asked.

"You mean Coleson? He might be an asshole, but he's not actually a bigot. Thankfully." Jack said. "I'd have reported him long ago if he was."

Jamie Sands

After a quick check of the stalls, Jack locked the door.

"You ready for this?" Emmaline said, licking her lips.

"Yeah, ready as I'll ever be."

Emmaline placed her hand on the glass of the mirror and did the same spell Jack had seen her do twice before now. It was becoming familiar, almost.

After a moment, Gerard's face appeared in the mirror. It was the more human-looking version of his face, his eyes were bright and blue and his forehead was clear of horns. "Em! Hello? Lucky you caught me I was just about to leave for a revel."

"Perfect, we're coming with you, me and Jack," Emmaline said.

He stared at her for a moment, his eyebrows drawing together and his mouth forming an O shape. She smiled back blandly and for a full minute no one said anything.

"I don't think you quite understand what you're asking," he said, slowly.

"A dark fey revel? The Wild Hunt will be there, right? We need to talk to them," Emmaline said.

"It's the last piece of the puzzle. Please, Gerard," Jack said. She moved beside Emmaline and gave Gerard a wave. His expression brightened a little, seeing her, and he gave her a finger wave back before shaking his head and frowning.

"But, a revel... it's not like – it's a rave, but not. It's worse than a student party turned up to eleven, there's blood and sex and all sorts of stuff. It's dangerous, too dangerous for you both. Humans die there, if they're not careful." He shrugged his shoulders. "Raphael's afraid to go to them."

Jamie Sands

"We have a reverend to retrieve," Jack said, she folded her arms. "He's an innocent victim in this whole mess."

Gerard looked between their two faces. After another minute, he relented. "Okay, I'll bring you through. But if you're coming to this thing with me there's some prep to do and a couple of rules, all right? It'll sound weird, but you have to trust me. If you don't do it, it'll be a million times worse. And I want to be on record as telling you both this is a bad idea and not to do it."

"Got it. You have a deal, you've warned us," Jack said. Emmaline nodded as well.

Gerard stepped part of the way through the mirror, offering a hand to them. Jack went first, climbing up on the bay of sinks and he helped her through into the living room of his house in Faerie. Emmaline followed close behind.

It looked and smelt just the same as the last time they'd

visited

Jack looked around, breathing in the weird scent of Faerie again. The living room was comfortingly familiar, although she was reminded that the last time she and Emmaline had been there together, when she'd told her they could never be more than friends.

Gerard closed the portal and looked at the two of them, frowning, one of his hands cupping his chin.

"Rules," he said, finally, dropping his hand to his side. "So, everything Raph will have warned you about but, like, times a thousand. There are incubus and succubus who go to the revels, they'll try to bind you to them. And you'll want to agree with them. And you don't want to want that."

He turned to a wooden chest and opened it before looking back at them again. "Questions?"

"Bind to them?" Jack asked.

"Yeah, like, uh... make a bargain which means you belong to them." Gerard's cheeks pinked prettily.

"Belong how?"

"Like, imagine you sold your soul to a demon and it could command you to do things, and magically, you'd kind of need to do those things," Gerard said. "Like that."

"Gotcha. Don't want bargains," Jack said. She rubbed her arm. Her stomach turned over and knotted itself.

"You said there'd be some prep?" Emmaline asked.

"I'm afraid the safest way for Jack to attend is by looking like she already belongs to someone, so they won't try to. Um. You know, steal her." He picked up a sturdy looking black leather collar and held it out to them. "So, you should wear this, and act like you, y'know, belong to Emmaline." He didn't look at either of them, obviously feeling awkward.

Jack eyed the collar then took it. "Yeah, I mean, she's the one with powers and spirits and stuff. I just have a baton and pepper spray and no magic at all."

"You should also probably leave all that here," Gerard said, apologetically. He looked around and picked up a small dagger and holster. "You could maybe get away with that."

Jack sighed and put her stick and pepper spray on the coffee table, then took the holster from Gerard. "What else?"

Gerard blushed deeper. "You ought to look more like you came to have fun, so. Um." He looked down at his own leather pants and pulled his white shirt open to reveal a leather chest harness, sitting snugly across his pectorals. Jack felt a slight blush on her own cheeks.

Jamie Sands

"Less clothes?" Emmaline asked, smiling. She was apparently quite comfortable with all these suggestions. Gerard nodded and she stripped off her scarf, shirt, boots, and socks, until she was wearing a thin black camisole and black boy-cut shorts.

Jack watched, feeling increasingly out of her depth. Or rather, like she was on the edge of a high-diving platform and the time to back up and go back down the ladder was rapidly passing.

She stared at all the skin Emmaline was showing, taking in the small tattoos scattered over her body. She was staring too long. Emmaline seemed to notice, too, because she smiled, pleased, and winked at her.

Jack tore her eyes away and looked down at herself, instead.

She peeled off her leather jacket and started unbuttoning her grey shirt, pulled it off and hung it over the back of a chair. Underneath, she wore a black sports bra. "This is all I have."

"I can probably make it a bit more, uh, impressive, if you don't mind?" Gerard asked. He took a step closer to her, looking at her critically.

"Sure, anything to blend in a little more. I trust you, Gerard." Jack smiled at Gerard, trying to cut through some of the awkwardness over the general... sexiness of the situation.

Not that she was attracted to Gerard, particularly, although he seemed to have a sort of aura around him. Emmaline's naked limbs, on the other hand, were imprinted on her memory.

Gerard smiled and placed a hand on her shoulder. Jack looked down at her chest and saw the shimmer of magic as her plain sports bra transformed into a black leather bra with too many straps. Her breasts weren't particularly big but they were pushed up and out in this thing. It was very flattering.

"There, much more dark fey," Gerard said. He moved back from her and stood next to Emmaline. "What do you think?"

"It's lovely," Emmaline said, staring wide eyed at her new piece of clothing.

Jack felt her cheeks warm even further.

"I'm leaving my pants and shoes on," she said. Bare feet seemed like a bridge too far, somehow.

"Fine, and you still have the string charms Raphael made you?" Gerard asked. He looked at their wrists and nodded to himself. "The safest thing for Jack would be if you bound her to you, Em, but of course it's up to the two of you."

Jack's heart skipped. Bound to her? Magically? That was definitely a bridge too far. "Uh, no. I'm all right."

"Collar, though," Emmaline said. She moved in front of Jack.

"Do you want me to put it on you?"

Jack opened her mouth but for a moment she couldn't speak.

This was getting close to some things she'd done with Marlo.

She had vivid memories of power games, misuse of her

police-issue handcuffs, even a collar a few times, but there

was no emotion attached to the memories. No arousal, no

affection, no sadness. It was odd. Jack could feel the absence

of what the memories meant.

Logically, Jack knew she couldn't belong to anyone again, it

wasn't good for her, or for the people around her.

But this was Emmaline. She was sweet, trustworthy, and kind.

Besides, this was part of the act they would put on to pass

through the dark fey. It was pretend, she told herself. All

pretend.

Jack nodded and handed her the collar. "Yeah, go for it."

Emmaline moved behind her to fasten the collar around her neck. She felt Emmaline's breath against her bare skin, and it seemed to send warmth down her spine, sparks of it spreading through her body and heating between her legs. She was already tense from the case, and from the being in Faerie, about to head into a dangerous unknown, but this was a more delicious tension.

One with the promise of pleasure behind it.

Had she felt this with Marlo? She could remember the first time Marlo had put a collar around her neck, but it was like she'd watched it in a movie. There were no feelings associated, just a curious emptiness. Like there was a hollow place in her heart. Without the memory of the emotions she felt inexperienced and vulnerable.

"Looks good on you," Emmaline said. She moved back around in front of Jack and adjusted the way the collar set on her throat. Jack flushed further, her breath quickening.

Whatever, they could deal with this later. They had a mission, and time was short. Hopefully, it wasn't already too late.

"Right, we're ready to get to the reverend," Jack said, trying to pull herself together. "Then we can deal with all of this."

Oh god, what had she just said? She shook her head, swallowed, and avoided Emmaline's gaze.

She ended up looking at Gerard. He ran both hands through his hair, from his forehead to the base of his skull. As he did this, his appearance changed. His eyes turned shiny and black and his horns sprouted out of his forehead. When he turned to hang up his shirt on a hook, she saw a strange twisted tattoo on his back. It looked like seaweed in a river, maybe.

"Gerard," Jack said, breathlessly. He was so eerie and pretty, she lost her train of thought. She wanted him to touch her, she wanted to kiss him.

"Are you all right?" He asked.

"Your aura," Emmaline said. "You're being all incubusy at her. Stop it."

"I can't help it, sorry," Gerard said. He looked away, and Jack shook her head, mortified with herself. Just the introduction of leather and she was all into everyone around her? No, it had to be Gerard's magic. It wasn't her fault, no need to have a sexual attraction crisis.

It was better when he wasn't looking at her directly. Damn, it was hot in the living room.

"What else do we need to know?" Jack said, her voice deliberately business-like.

"Do you want me to go with you?" Gerard asked.

"It'd be safest, if you could," Emmaline said. "But we can probably handle it. I have magic and Jack basically beat up Timaris for information."

"Well, I'll come with as long as I can, but if Farren's around – and I expect him to be – I might need to take off. You know, go to him," Gerard said. He reached a hand up to rub the back of his neck, where a collar similar to Jack's appeared at the mere mention of Farren.

"Farren?" Jack asked.

"His kelpie," Emmaline said, smiling affectionately at Gerard. "His master."

"He asked me to be there tonight, so I should get there soon," Gerard said. He looked at the both of them and nodded. "You two ready for this?"

Jamie Sands

"As ready as I can be," Jack said.

45

"This is like the sequence in that Kubrick movie. You know, with the rich people party," Jack said. "All those white people writhing together with masks on."

"Do you mean *Eyes Wide Shut?*" Gerard asked.

"Yes," Jack said. "Only in this version, it's not all white people."

"And it's not all people," Emmaline said. She took hold of Jack's hand and squeezed it. Jack was grateful for the connection. And not just because she was feeling all kinds of attraction to her.

The forest here was different to the one they'd seen before. This one was eerie, made of a lot of twisted trees. Some formed into benches, bending their branches into tunnels and arches. Here and there were statues and strange animals peering out from the undergrowth. There were beds of soft-looking green moss and strange purple and red flowers giving off a scent unlike anything Jack had smelt before. Something sweet and intoxicating.

All over the path and beyond, under the trees, on the moss, and in the long grasses, fey of all kinds were tangled up together kissing, having sex, and everything in between. A lot were coupling, which was possibly a bad choice of word, Jack thought, because very few of them were just one on one. Having sex in every way Jack had ever imagined and also a number of ways she'd never considered on account of never having a partner with tentacles, claws, or a tail.

She stopped walking, distracted by a blue glowing pixie with huge wings. She was beautiful, curvaceous, and tall. She was clearly getting off on having her wings stroked by a twiggy, tree-looking being with long stringy hair like weeping willow leaves.

"This way," Gerard said.

Emmaline tugged on Jack's hand, pulling her down the path. Jack wiped her mouth with the back of her other hand and focused on the way Emmaline's hair moved in her ponytail, and not on the fey getting off.

"There." Gerard pointed towards a tall and twisty tree with fluffy purple leaves.

Jack recognised Timaris under the tree, dancing around a squirming young man with several other fey creatures. The dance looked like some perversion of a maypole as they bound him to the tree with thorny vines.

"Oh," Emmaline said. Something in the breathy way she said it made Jack glance at her face. Her cheeks were flushed, and her eyes were wide.

"Shit, I have to go," Gerard said. "Sorry. I see Farren and he has a look in his eye. Sorry again."

"We'll be okay," Emmaline said. She shook her head slightly and took a deep breath. "Go see him. We'll talk to who we need to and go straight back to your house. The path leads the way, yes?"

"Yes. I'll be back as soon as I can." Gerard backed away towards a tall, beautiful man in clothes so deep green they looked black. His skin was pale, almost glowing green and grey, his hair a thick sheet of dark curls. His eyes were sunken and dark, seeming to flash as he caught sight of Gerard and a smile touched his lips.

Jack thought of a deep pond near one of the houses she'd lived in as a child. Her father had warned her on threat of extremely severe punishment not to go near it. Of course it had been a huge temptation, after the warning. But she never had gone close to the pond. There was too much fear of her father and of the unknown in her, then.

How things had changed.

"What did you say Gerard's master was?" Jack asked, watching as the man reached out to Gerard and Gerard took his hand. They moved back into the shadows as the man wrapped his arms around Gerard and pulled him close into his chest. It was a sweet gesture, or it would have been, if they weren't both dark fey...

"He's a kelpie, a water horse," Emmaline said, swallowing hard and tearing her eyes away from where Gerard had vanished into the shadows. "They drown and eat people."

"But he was a man, not a horse."

"Sorry, yes. He's a shapeshifter," Emmaline said. She squeezed her hand. "Kelpies are shapeshifters. Not everyone would be tempted by a fine-looking horse."

Jamie Sands

"How are we getting out of this?" Jack asked softly, before she thought it through. She had meant to continue to be brave outwardly.

But now, she'd let Emmaline know she was unsure. She shivered from the top of her head to her toes. She felt raw, bare-skinned and vulnerable, highly aware that she, as a human, was at the bottom of the food chain here.

"I'll keep you safe," Emmaline said. She dropped her hand and took hold of Jack's wrist instead. Then she stepped off the path towards the Wild Hunt, towing Jack behind her.

Emmaline's hand around her wrist was comforting, more so than she expected it to be – the warm feel of her hand around her wrist, the aura of power Jack could feel vibrating off her in the magical atmosphere.

Jack stood up straighter as they approached the fey.

"Timaris, we need to talk," Emmaline said.

The fey stopped dancing. All of them turned to look at Jack and Emmaline. The man being lashed to the tree squirmed and whimpered, his eyes squeezed closed.

Timaris dropped the end of the vine he was holding and approached the two of them, one eyebrow perfectly arched.

"Well, hello there, little mage and little human, how can Timaris serve you today?" He asked, slightly out of breath from the dance.

"Did he consent to this?" Jack asked. Her eyes riveted on the points of blood on the man's biceps and chest. Timaris followed her gaze and nodded.

"He begged for it, love. But I suspect he's not why you're here." Timaris's voice was amused, wheedling.

Jack kept her eyes on the man's face until he met her eyes and nodded slightly, concurring. He was into it. He moaned softly, more in pleasure than pain. Jack forced her gaze back onto Timaris's face.

"You were contracted to take a man from a church by Deacon or Eddy, right?" Jack said.

Timaris shrugged, showing off every one of his pointed teeth in a horrible smile. "Sounds vaguely familiar. Maybe, perhaps."

"Where is he?" Jack asked through gritted teeth.

A beautiful pixie approached and draped her arm around Timaris's shoulder. "Timmy, who are these two? Do they want to join the game?"

Jack looked into the pixie's sparkling indigo eyes. The word 'yes' rose in her chest. Her shoulders relaxed, she blinked slower, and smiled.

"Merredy," Timaris said in a sing-song voice. "These are some friends I made." He stroked a finger over the tattoo of Jack's feelings, fondly. "Leave them alone."

"The dark one is going to say yes to me," Merredy said. She said it so softly Jack thought maybe she'd heard her voice in her head. Had Merredy's mouth even moved?

"No, she isn't." Emmaline pulled Jack behind her, shielding her from the fey.

Jack had a sensation like she was too many cups of champagne into a wedding reception. She could hear Merredy and Timaris laughing from far away – much further away than they surely were.

"The man from the church," Emmaline said. "I want answers, and I'll give you some emotions as payment."

"What if we don't want emotions?" Merredy asked. Jack peered over Emmaline's shoulders and saw Merredy was still looking at her. Jack ducked back behind Emmaline. "What if we want something more?"

"He wants emotions." Jack could feel Emmaline raise her arm and point at Timaris. "He wants something juicy, like, say, the fear my brothers will be hurt, or maybe the hurt I have from when people say I'm evil because I have an affinity for the deathly arts."

"Oh yes, I want those!" Timaris said. He sounded excited. Jack thought about little kids at the gift shop of a theme park, begging for toys. "I want *thoooose*."

Jack's legs felt wobbly. She draped an arm around Emmaline's waist and leaned her cheek on her shoulder blade. Emmaline smelt good. How had Jack not noticed how good Emmaline smelt? Fresh, floral, more anchoring than the air here with the strange sweetness to it.

"Emmaline, I feel weird," she murmured.

"It's the hunt," she replied. "Merredy has a pheromone or something. Just, try and focus. Think of something boring from back home."

"Urgh, fine," Merredy said. "Timmy will deal with you."

Emmaline wound one arm around Jack to help hold her up, Jack leaned heavily against her. "Close your eyes, pet," she said. "And keep them closed."

"Aeva's grandmother." Jack murmured, trying to warn Emmaline.

She did as she was told and leaned on her, enjoying the warmth of her body. She lost track of time and of what was happening. The darkness behind her eyelids was so interesting here. It was velvety blue and there were small flecks of lights chasing each other around. Jack giggled as she watched them, like tiny shooting stars. She could hear voices in the distance, but she ignored them.

Jamie Sands

Emmaline nudged Jack with her hip. "Eyes open again, Jack. It's time to go."

"Time to?" Jack opened her eyes and blinked at Em... Emmy, she felt blurry, like she'd been asleep. "Is it done?"

"Mm-hmm, look," Em smiled and raised her other hand, which was clasped in the hand of a bewildered looking Reverend Zebedee.

"It's the rev!" Jack said, laughing.

"Where am I? Detective Jack, is that you?" he asked.

The fey had moved back, turning towards the tree. Jack's heart thudded as she watched them, and she wasn't sure if it was because she was disappointed or relieved they hadn't tried to kidnap her.

Both.

Maybe mostly relieved, though. When Merredy turned away, Jack's head began to clear again. Whatever that fey had, it was intoxicating.

"This way, the both of you," Emmaline said, tugging them both towards the path and back towards Gerard's house. Her grip was firm on Jack's hand, reassuring and solid.

"I thought..." Jack saw a group of feminine-looking scaly fish fey in a rushing river, kissing and fondling each other. There was a human there with them, moving slowly. The fishy people were pressing their body down as they kissed.

How many missing persons would she find here? And from how many countries? Surely, this wasn't just New Zealand's little bit of fairyland.

Em tugged on her. "Jack, focus. You were thinking, what? Tell me," she said.

"I was thinking," Jack looked at Em. "You can go to another place, right? The death place?"

"Yes, the other side of life. Or, the spirit world, depending on how you look at things," Emmaline said.

"Isn't getting back to Earth the same?" Jack asked.

Em tilted her hand. "Maybe. I've never tried. I mean, I've been to Faerie as often as you have."

There was a scream from somewhere nearby. Jack's head whipped around to look for the source. Her head spun a little. She scanned the area but there were so many people, fey, and human, and things she couldn't recognise. And some of the forms were actually trees and some of the trees were fey, too. It was too much.

The reverend was staring at some statues situated on the side of the path. Some of them looked too lifelike to be carved. Some of them were old, weathered, and broken; some of them looked quite new.

"What are these?" Jack asked.

"I don't know," Emmaline said. Then she frowned. "I think I can feel death on them. These were human once."

"Don't leave the path," Jack breathed. One of the newest ones looked almost familiar. She peered into the face, half recognising it. One of her cases? One of the unsolved ones? Her mind felt mushy still.

"Who are you?" she asked the statue.

"Those are fairies, right?" Zebedee said, as if he were waking from a nightmare. "Fairies. I'm in the land of the fairies."

"Okay, let's all be quiet. No more questions, focus on walking, stay on the path," Emmaline said, and hurried her pace. "And hopefully we'll get the fuck out of here."

46

In Gerard's house, Jack sat on the couch and didn't move until her head cleared. Then she pulled her shirt back on, reaching up to undo the leather collar. She turned it around in her hands and put it on the table. Her bra was still leather and she guessed it was going to stay that way. She sort of didn't mind that. Gerard had made it rather comfortable somehow.

The reverend was shaken but not totally confused. Jack thought he wasn't surprised so much about the existence of fairies and travel between dimensions.

Emmaline had given him a once-over and couldn't find any injuries on him, although he had no idea what had happened to him. He sat in the armchair across the room, rubbing his forehead with one hand.

"I can remember being out the back of the church. I have a place where I leave offerings," he said. "Bowls of milk for the brownies."

"I've seen you do it," Jack said. "I thought you had a cat."

"I was out the back there, and I'd stopped to check on the monarch caterpillars on my milkweed. I heard laughter and felt hands on me. Then I – no. Then, it's blackness," he said. He rubbed his eyes and sighed, sitting back on the couch and resting his head. He looked exhausted.

"They said you vanished in the middle of choir practise," Jack said. "We have the whole choir swearing to it."

"Probably an illusion," Emmaline said, bringing in a cup of tea for the reverend. "They could have already taken him but sent a shadow of him to attend choir, for maximum confusion and drama. Or a shapeshifter."

"My poor choir," he said. He took the teacup and brought it close to his face, inhaling the steam.

"But why make him disappear in plain sight?" Jack asked. "It was the number one way to raise the most suspicion, I'd have thought Deacon and Eddy would want him to quietly vanish."

"It won't have been them, it was the hunt that took him," Emmaline said. She walked the room, as if she were too restless to sit down. "And yeah, it makes no sense, but they're fey and they won't have any real-world consequences. Some of them feed off emotions, so the confusion and fear would be like a bonus to them. They wouldn't have even considered what it'd mean for Deacon. Or if they did, they liked the chaos of it all."

"I don't remember any of it," Zebedee said. He sipped the tea and made a satisfied sound.

"That could be for the best," Jack said.

Emmaline looked at the mirror and traced a finger over it. "Jack's right. I'm sure you'll get snatches and hints of it back in nightmares, maybe. You're probably better off not knowing."

Zebedee sighed and sat back, sipping at the tea. "You could be right. Listen, thank you both so much for coming to get me. Really, from the bottom of my heart, I'm grateful."

"It's all right," Jack said, she managed a smile for the old man. "You were an innocent victim. What's my job if not to rescue people?"

Zebedee smiled at her and nodded. "I understand. You're driven to bring justice."

"At least I could save you," Jack said. She thought back to the face she'd almost recognised transmuted into a statue on the side of the path and shivered. "I can't always."

Jamie Sands

"I think I can do this, I think I can get us back through the mirror," Emmaline said. Her hand pressed flat on the glass. "It's not so different from leaving the realm of Death, and besides, this mirror's been used to go between worlds so much it almost knows how to do it itself."

"Wonderful," Jack said. She felt emptied out, and bone tired. She could probably sleep right here on the couch. Zebedee set his cup down and got up, giving Jack an encouraging smile.

"I'd very much like to get home and have a bath," he said. "And if that involves a mirror, I'm fine with that."

Jack hauled herself up from the couch and nodded. "Lead on, Em."

Emmaline flashed her a sweet smile and started the incantation.

47

"So, let me get this straight." Sergeant Apanui flipped through the paperwork and closed the file. "The mysterious disappearance of Edith Armstrong. It was all related to how her son allegedly killed her daughter's lover twenty years ago?"

Jack and Piper stood before her desk, Jack hoping her own confidence was hiding Piper's nervousness.

"Right," Jack said, she clasped her hands behind her back and recited the story Piper, Emmaline, and she had settled on. "Eddy faked his own death and went into hiding. He recently hired some gang members, using Aeva as an intermediary, to muddy up the trail and conceal himself. The gang removed Edith from her home using the spare key. Using the information, they extorted from Daniel's boyfriend, threatening to out him to his conservative family. He told them about the key and the schedule Edith kept. When they took her, they set it up to look like a locked-room mystery. In fact, it was straight forward."

The sergeant raised an eyebrow and fixed Jack with a sceptical look. Jack continued.

"So, it's all wrapped up. Edith's not pressing charges against Eddy, but the crown is. Depending on how the court case goes it could be restorative justice or jail time, but you know that, of course. Joe doesn't want to charge Deacon for the extortion, but Deacon's offered money as compensation," Jack said. "Piper will appear in court to argue for community service and restorative justice."

"Community service is the best they can hope for, the girl, too, for helping them." Apanui patted the top of the file, nodded and looked up at Jack and Piper. "This is some good work. Thank you, Duarte."

"Of course, Sergeant. Also, I have the claim sheet for the time Emmaline Perrone put into this case. She was invaluable to getting it unravelled." Jack put the form on her desk.

"Fine," Apanui said, taking the sheet and adding it to a separate pile. "I'll sign it off and give it to payroll today. Jack, tell me one thing." Apanui gave Jack an appraising look. Jack shifted her weight from one foot to the other. "You're not putting yourself in undue danger, are you?"

"Not at all," Jack lied. "You know me, I'm cautious."

"And Piper, how did they do?"

Piper, who was standing right next to Jack, made a tiny squeaky noise. There was silence for a moment after. Jack gathered her thoughts before responding.

"Piper was fantastic. I'm impressed with their attention to detail, their initiative when on their own, and their ability to connect with people really helped with questioning," Jack said, meaning every word. She was pleased to realise that she genuinely valued Piper and wanted to continue working with them.

"You're happy to work together from now on, the both of you?" Apanui looked between Jack and Piper, her eyebrows raised.

Piper looked to Jack, who gave them a quick smile. They licked their lips and then nodded. "Yes please, ma'am."

Jack nodded and grinned. "Absolutely. There's just one last thing. I'd like to file an official complaint about Detective Coleson. He obstructed our investigation on more than one occasion, and he harassed Piper."

Apanui frowned, leaned over to her filing cabinet, and pulled out a sheaf of papers. "I'll need you to fill out some forms."

Jack drove Piper home. They were over the moon, babbling with excitement in the car's back seat.

"I can't wait until our next case! Do you think it'll be something else with the fey? Or some other weird thing?" Piper asked.

"I really don't know," Jack said, glancing up to meet Piper's eyes in the rear view mirror. "We'll have to wait and see what lands in our laps, I suppose."

"And Emmaline will be involved too, right?" Piper said, leaning forward to squeeze Emmaline's shoulder.

"If she wants to be," Jack said. She glanced at Emmaline, smiling, despite herself. Her heart fluttered a little, remembering the night before in Faerie.

Jamie Sands

"I want to be," Emmaline said, nodding. "I've travelled too much lately. I want to settle for a little bit, be somewhere Raphael can find me easily. Try and track down my other brother, maybe."

"I guess we have a team," Jack said. "Assuming Apanui signs off on your consultancy fee."

"Yay, a squad!" Emmaline said.

"A crew," Piper said. "But not like Taylor Swift's one because none of us are tall, leggy models."

"And I'm fine with that. I do not need to be Taylor Swift," Jack said. She pulled the car into the car park out the front of Piper's house. "You did good work, rookie. Sleep in tomorrow. For real, this time."

"I'm gonna move house," Piper said, airily. "So you don't know where it is and you can't knock on my door."

"Wise choice," Jack nodded.

"And hey," Piper said, a little more seriously. They pushed the door of the car open but didn't get out. "Thanks for that complaint stuff with Coleson."

"No worries," Jack said. "I should've done it earlier."

"Do you think it'll change things?" Piper asked.

Jack sucked her teeth. "I don't know. Apanui will talk to him, I'm sure. Whether or not he's bright enough to listen is another question. Either way, the complaint is on record now."

Piper nodded and got out of the car. Their smile faded. "See you tomorrow."

"Sleep well."

Emmaline was quiet in the car for most of the drive back to Jack's place.

Jamie Sands

"Is this what it's normally like, at the end of a case?" Emmaline asked.

"Well," Jack shrugged one shoulder. "This one was a bit on the, uh, complicated side. It'll feel more real and settled after the case goes through court."

"Seriously," Emmaline nodded. "It's still exciting, though, getting all the ends tied up."

Jack parked round the back of her building in the usual spot. Marlo was waiting outside the front door in a black sheath dress and heels. Her red-painted lips were stretched wide in a plasticky grin.

"For fuck's sake, Marlo," Jack muttered, shaking her head. "Can't you take a hint?"

Marlo's smile faltered when she saw Emmaline get out of Jack's car.

"Jacky, who's this?" Marlo looked Emmaline up and down, her nose wrinkling.

"Doesn't matter," Jack said. "Marlo, go ahead and leave. The fact of the matter is I don't want you in my life. You're no good for me, and I'm confident I'm not good for you, either."

Marlo blinked slowly, then turned her head and spat on the ground. "You replaced me did you? This little blonde piece of fluff? She looks like a teenager."

"I'm twenty-three," Emmaline grumbled.

"For fuck's sake, it's not about replacing you," Jack said. She gritted her teeth and looked directly into Marlo's eyes. "It's about how whatever we had between us is over, and you need to stop calling me and stop coming around or I'll file a restraining order. You understand?"

Marlo took a half step back and eyed Emmaline scornfully. "Jacky you don't mean–"

Jamie Sands

"Oh my goddess, listen to her," Emmaline said, losing her temper. She stormed forward and Marlo took another half step back. "She said no to you about ten different ways. Get the hint!"

Jack smirked, took Emmaline's hand, and walked past Marlo. "Go, Marlo. Don't come back. Go to counselling and talk through your issues, will you?"

Marlo slunk away into the dusk.

49

Emmaline's heart thumped quickly as they went into Jack's apartment. She smiled as Jack put the bolt and the chain on the door and ran her hand through her hair. She was nervous.

If that was Jack's ex, she knew Jack couldn't possibly see her as a romantic partner. Marlo had been right about one thing – Emmaline couldn't replace Marlo. She was half as tall, her breasts weren't as impressive as Marlo's, and she had none of her sophisticated fashion sense.

She should probably find somewhere else to stay. Jack had said that who Emmaline was didn't matter... But did she really think that?

Jack walked into the house, hung her jacket on a hook on the wall, and went into the kitchen. Emmaline trailed behind, feeling uncertain.

"I'm sorry you had to see all that," Jack said, sighing.

"She was your ex, wasn't she? The one you traded your love for to Timaris."

"Yeah." Jack avoided her eyes. Emmaline leaned back against the kitchen counter and folded her arms.

"You're lucky if the fey only took your love for her. They might've taken more than they said they would. They might've taken all your love. All the love you're capable of feeling." Emmaline's heart twisted a little at the thought of it. She hoped it wasn't so, but there would be no way to know…

"I mean, maybe I'm better off without love," Jack said. She opened the pantry and pulled out a box of cat biscuits. "Marlo and I, our relationship got pretty unhealthy."

"Don't say that," Emmaline said, her heart twisting further. "Everyone needs love. Otherwise, you'd die a lot faster."

"Did you read that in an article?" Jack asked, her voice dry.

"No, it's a fact. I know about death, and I know about life. Love is sustaining."

There was a thump at the window and Jack turned to open it and let in an orange cat, who stalked in and complained loudly. Jack smiled as it pushed its head against her hand.

"Okay, okay. I'll get you some sardines since you're clearly starving to death," Jack said, smiling indulgently at the cat.

Emmaline watched Jack put away the cat biscuits and pull out a small tin. She hooked the fishes out of the tin with a fork and mashed them into a bowl.

As she worked, she told the cat how pretty it was, and how she was sorry she hadn't been home so much lately.

"That's settled, then," Emmaline said once the cat was happily eating.

"What's settled?" Jack asked. She wiped her hands with a tea towel patterned with native flowers of New Zealand.

"They didn't take all your love, or you wouldn't have cared about the cat."

"Huh, maybe so." Jack tipped her head to one side and shrugged. "So, um, here's a pretty safe place for you. In terms of not being tracked down by the Order of Mage Hunters, right?"

"Yes? I mean it's still early days but it's harder for them to operate in a busier area like this. You're good protection, too." Emmaline wrapped her arms around herself and hoped very hard the hunters couldn't find her here.

"Well. How about we go to your place and pick up the rest of your stuff," Jack said.

"You mean...?" Emmaline swallowed and blinked. "Do you want me to stay?"

"It makes sense, if you're going to stick around and help out with my cases. Besides, the spare room sits empty most of the time, I'd just have to clear some stuff out. My dad only comes to stay once a year at Christmas. He can take my room, and I'll sleep on the couch." Jack had clearly thought this through, which was unexpected and pretty sweet.

Em swallowed again, uncertain. "It makes sense, sure. But do you want me to stay? Like, you actually want me around. Me?"

Jack looked as if she was fighting a battle inside her head and then she sucked in her breath. "Yes. I want you to stay. Please move in with me."

"Like, as a flatmate?" Emmaline licked her lips, uncertain but hopeful.

"You saw my ex, so you know I'm a bit of a train wreck." Jack breathed out, a flicker of several different emotions crossing her face. "But, maybe, we can be more than work acquaintances in the long run. Or maybe flatting won't work out and I'll have to kick you out, I just don't know."

"So, friends?" Emmaline's heart fluttered with a hope she hardly dared to feel.

"Friends to start with," Jack said, slowly. "And, maybe, with time, we could try out something else. Something more than that, I don't know. We just met, it feels like, but... it also feels like I've known you for ages – years, maybe. You'll have to be patient with me, I'm afraid. So, do you want to move in?"

Emmaline waited for a moment to double check she hadn't imagined it. Jack's expression was raw, vulnerable. As open and afraid as when she'd been under the influence of the pixie from the Wild Hunt.

"Of course, I'd love to. But I need you to want this, not just because I want this," Emmaline said. Her heart was thudding now, her pulse loud in her ears.

"Oh. Right. Yes, I want this."

Emmaline launched herself at Jack and wrapped her arms around her, laughing. Jack hugged her back and Emmaline heard her laughing softly, too.

This felt right.

"Let's go get my stuff."

End

Acknowledgments

Thanks to Ellen Boucher for being my Britishness consultant

Thanks also to all the people who beta read this one over the years, especially Liz, who has an endless capacity to put up with shittty drafts. To Court, for your brilliant creative input, co-creation of some of the characters and your constant friendship. And a huge thank you to Ada and Rookery Publishing for taking a chance on this weird little genre-fluid story and for believing in Detective Duarte and Piper.

And of course, big thanks to my partner, Anna, always.

About the Author

Jamie Sands grew up in Wellington, the capital city of New Zealand. As a child they were a library devotee and were always reading something (even if it was just Roald Dahl's The Witches over and over and over.) This translated quickly into a love of story telling and creative writing. Always fascinated with monsters, Magic and weirdness, these things often bled through into their stories.

As an adult, their fiction ranges over many genre, including horror, young adult, romantic comedy and urban fantasy. They have self published roleplaying games as well as queer romance under a pen name (Jaxon Knight).

Jamie moved to Auckland at the very end of 2014 and has lived there since with their wife and a round cat named Mochi.

Jamie Sands

This strange city of oceans and volcanoes has become their home although Wellington will always have a place in their heart.

Jamie studied English literature at Victoria University of Wellington, including a Summer course on poetry taught by Gregory O'Brien. Their young adult novel the Suburban Book of the Dead was nominated for a Sir Julius Vogel award in 2019. Their queer romance has been reviewed on the Big Gay Fiction Podcast.

As part of the Rainbow Romance Writers of New Zealand group, Jamie champions inclusion and diversity in fiction. The group is comprised of writers from all over the country who write romance in which queer characters find their happy ever after.

The Detective Duarte series is their first foray into women who love women novels.

Also by Jamie Sands

Overdues and Occultism

The Suburban Book of the Dead

Honeymoon in Japan

Fairyland Romances

(As Jaxon Knight)

Rival Princes

Mischief and Mayhem

Recipe for Chaos

The Good, the Bad and the Dad

New Year's Eve (Fairyland Stories Book 1)